SHIVA'S CHALLENGE

SHIVA'S CHALLENGE

AN ADVENTURE OF THE ICE AGE

J. H. BRENNAN

HarperCollins*Publishers*

Shiva's Challenge
An Adventure of the Ice Age
Copyright © 1992 by J. H. Brennan

1   2   3   4   5   6   7   8   9   10
First Edition

Library of Congress Cataloging-in-Publication Data
Brennan, J. H.
  Shiva's challenge: an adventure of the Ice Age /
by J. H. Brennan
      p.   cm.
  Summary: Fourteen-year-old Shiva submits to an ordeal in the frozen wasteland north of her tribe's camp, to test her potential for becoming shaman for the Shingu people. Sequel to "Shiva" and "Shiva Accused."
  ISBN 0-06-020825-2. — ISBN 0-06-020826-0 (lib. bdg.)
  [1. Man, Prehistoric—Fiction.]   I. Title.
PZ7.B75155Si   1992   91-40676
[Fic]—dc20   CIP
                                                                        AC

Contents

SHIVA'S CHALLENGE

1

Ordeal by Poison

They came for her in the darkness hours.

Shiva awoke at once, her heart racing. The faces of the women stared grimly down at her, caught in the flickering firelight. Each was painted white, with streaks of red across the mouth and with eyes rimmed black, like the faces of demons.

"What's wrong?" Shiva whispered.

They took her arms, half dragged her to her feet. She had been sleeping alone, away from the house of women, as young people sometimes did, sheltered by a rocky overhang, in the pool of warmth provided by a glowing ringfire. No one spoke.

"What's wrong?" Shiva asked again. These were women of her tribe—she recognized Eena and Elder Looca, even beneath the paint—but she felt very much afraid. She had never before seen women painted in this manner. Besides, there was threat in the air, chill as fog, so clearly present she could almost taste it.

She looked around in growing panic. The ring-fires still burned high near the booma thorn fence, protecting the Shingu tribe from predators and spirits of the night. But there were no guards nearby; and if there had been, Shiva did not think they would have aided her.

It was brutally cold. Winter had come early, and Mamar's breath ripped down from the northlands, blocking the passes with snow so that the tribe could not move south. It had happened before. Young as she was, even Shiva could remember its happening on two occasions. On one of them Mamar had relented, a single pass had opened and the tribe had moved south belatedly. On the other they had remained trapped throughout the winter, their hunters forced to brave the snowfields. Many had died that year. The cold they felt now would not be the worst of it. Later there would be no wood for the ring-fires, no thorn bushes for the booma.

They pulled her forward, stumbling. There were close on a dozen women; and now that the sleep cloud had lifted from her mind, Shiva recognized others among them, including two more elders, but no one she knew well.

"Where are you taking me?" she demanded. But still they did not answer.

Was she accused of crime? Once before, she had been taken like this, brought to trial and condemned. But that had been by women of another tribe. Her own people, the Shingu, had always treated her well, even as an orphan child. Later, when she found the skull of Saber, she was respected by all her tribe. She knew of nothing she had done to warrant different treatment now.

The tribe had made camp, following Chief Renka's instructions, on an area of rocky flatland in the foothills, hopeful of a change of weather. But there had been no change yet. Even now, as they took her past the longhouse, flurries of snow blew into her face, and a knife edge in the gusting wind almost took her breath away.

"Please," Shiva whispered, "where are you taking me?"

"Quiet, girl!" Elder Looca told her sternly. She had a deep voice, like a man's, made rough by age.

Another of the elders stepped forward: a slight, sharp-faced woman by the name of Yste. She carried furred strips twisted in one hand. By the smell, Shiva knew they had been cut from the pelt of a black bear, recently killed. She felt a chill deeper than the biting cold. The slaughter of the bear would have been easy: The great creatures had long since curled up for their winter sleep. But to reach it, someone would have had to venture into the forbidden caves; and the bear, besides, was totem to the tribal Crones. Those strips in Yste's hands meant only one thing: There was magic here. Shiva shuddered.

Two of the women, whose names she did not know, pulled her arms behind her and crossed them at the wrists. From somewhere on her left, toward the east, she heard the rhythmic click of bone on bone and the eerie wail of a shaman's reed. In the half dark beyond the ringfire she saw shadows move. Softly, so softly it might have been imagination, there came the sonorous monotony of Cronechant.

Yste tied her wrists using the twisted strips of bearskin. Then, before Shiva quite realized what was happening, she took a broader strip and wrapped it swiftly around her head in a blindfold. The skin had not been smoked and had been only roughly scraped, so it smelled of blood and bear. Shiva felt a thick ooze trickle down her cheek as Yste pulled it tight.

6

She could see nothing. The bindings left her completely blind—not even a hint of ringfire light crept through. But she could hear well enough. As she listened, pictures formed in her mind. The shadow shapes to the east resolved themselves into fur-clad warrior women, their faces painted like those who had seized her. They moved toward her in a shuffle dance. Her ears told her they were shaking spirit rattles.

Hands gripped her arms and pushed her forward. She was instantly surrounded by the warriors. The dry rasp of the rattles was everywhere. She could hear the shuffling footfalls. A woman's voice cried out shrilly in the ancient evocation of the ancestors.

Urged by the hands, Shiva walked, stumbling, across rough ground. She was increasingly confused, no longer certain of her position in the camp—or even if she was still in the camp at all. Her nose twitched. Like most of her tribe she had a keen sense of smell, and while the scent of bear was strong on the bindings, she still sensed other, subtler scents beyond it. They let her know at once that Renka, the tribal chief, was nearby, and with her, others of the elder council.

The rhythmic clicking sounds came closer. She heard the shuffling footsteps on the rocky ground.

The noises soon surrounded her, and she imagined dark figures in a circle dance, bobbing like huge birds against the backdrop of the firelight.

The sound of the shaman's reed grew louder, underpinned by a soft, trilling ululation that was somehow more sinister than the cough of a cave lion or the hissed warning of a snake. It was an announcement, the most dreaded announcement of them all.

The Crone approached.

Shiva saw her in her mind's eye as clearly as if Yste had removed the blindfold from her face. The Shingu Crone was ancient now, older even than Looca, who was oldest of the elders. Yet the Crone bore herself erect as a reed, the totem bearskin wrapped around her like a cloak. She was not merely Crone now, but Crone of Crones, the Hag whose hands clutched the destinies of all the tribes. As such, she was the most powerful witch in all the world. Shiva feared her as she feared no other living creature.

All sound stopped. Shiva's forward momentum halted. In the sudden silence she could clearly hear the breathing of those who stood around her and feel their body heat. There was a movement behind her; then the blindfold was removed.

They had taken her to a place beyond the

camp, between two hills, rugged with rocks and barren even of the stunted shrubs that grew throughout the foothills. There were fires lighted here, like the ringfires of the camp. Rank on rank, the tribe's women were drawn up watching, all faces painted deathly white. There were many she knew, yet none smiled at her. She found herself looking around, almost desperately, for Hiram, then realized there were no Shingu males here. For some reason the discovery worried her further. What was afoot that only the women must know?

The trilling started up again, and two girls younger than Shiva herself walked into the firelight, their bodies draped with strings of juju shells collected from some distant shore. Behind them, exactly as she had imagined, walked the Crone.

The Crone glanced toward her, black eyes glittering in the firelight. She wore, as Shiva had known she must wear, the full skin of a black bear. In life the beast had been twice her size and more, yet its pelt was folded with such cunning that it seemed to fit the witch as if she had grown into it.

Led by the trilling girls, the Crone walked slowly to a natural table in the center of the clearing, its smooth rock surface set just a little higher than her waist. She gestured, and those surrounding Shiva surged forward, carrying Shiva with them until she too stood by the table, directly facing the Crone across its surface. *What was happening? Why was she here?* The questions rose in her mind but stuck in her throat. She was afraid to ask. She stood transfixed, fascinated as bird prey by the power of a snake.

Around them, the women began to chant, a vibrating contralto sound that rose up like a swarm of summer bees. Feet stamped in unison while the renewed click of bone on bone provided a rhythmic counterpoint. Caught up in the rhythm of the chant, it was all Shiva could do to prevent herself from swaying. The Crone watched her, face expressionless.

The chanting stopped. For an instant there was silence more deafening than any sound. Then, to Shiva's horror, the Crone threw back her head and emitted a high-pitched call, half scream, half howl, that echoed like the nightwing's cry through the surrounding hills.

At once six masked women trotted from the darkness, each carrying a smallish bowl cut—as far as Shiva could determine—from a badger's skull. Her nose told her instantly the bowls were full. Plant scents, heady, rank and strange, rose from them in a sullen perfume. The women placed the bowls in a single line on the surface of the rock table before the Crone. They bowed, then danced away, sinuous as snakes beneath their furs.

Not once had the Crone's eyes left Shiva's face. Now she said quietly, "Release her hands."

Someone stepped forward and removed the twisted strips of bearskin. Shiva might have run then, but she did not. She was held by the power of the Crone's gaze, which was as strong as any bonds. Besides, where was there to run? Caught in the northlands in winter, she would be dead if she left the tribe.

The Crone's glance flickered downward to the skull bowls. Her voice was soft as the dry rustle of dead leaves. "Six bowls," she said. "All but one contain poison. Thus five are deadly; one is harmless." She looked back into Shiva's eyes and blinked once, slowly, like a reptile. "Drink!"

It was the Ordeal by Poison! The victim took one bowl and drank. If the Mother Goddess aided her, she chose the right bowl and survived. If not, she drank the poison and died a hideously agonizing death. Shiva had heard talk of the Ordeal before, but not like this. Always she had

11

been told it was convened only to try one convicted of murder by the Elder Council, and even then only rarely. Did they think her a murderess?

"Lady Witch—" Shiva began, heart thumping.

But the Crone cut her off. "Drink!" she whispered again, with such fierce authority that Shiva's hand reached out toward the bowls.

With a massive effort Shiva stopped herself, controlled the fear in her veins, the pounding of her heart. She met the Crone's gaze with every ounce of courage she possessed. "Why?" she whispered, so quietly that only the Crone could hear her. "Why is this being done to me?"

Impassively, the Crone stared back at her. "It is your destiny," she said.

Shiva felt her hand move again, driven by an irresistible compulsion. *Which bowl?* All looked alike. Their contents, dark, fluid, thick and viscous in the the firelight, looked alike and smelled alike. *Which bowl?* From only one might she drink safely and survive. Five were filled with death. *Which bowl?*

There were no sounds at all around her now. Even the night creatures seemed to have stilled their cries, as if they were congregated in the outer darkness, watching. What had she done? Why did the Crone speak of her destiny?

Even in her terror, Shiva's mind was filled with a vivid memory. She was standing surrounded by angry people of the Barradik tribe, condemned to death by stoning. She had been afraid then, as terrified as she was now, but she had determined she would show no weakness.

She made the same vow now, although confusion and bewilderment compounded her fear. The Crone said this was her destiny, and the Crone knew all things—and especially all things pertaining to destiny. So be it. If it was her destiny, she would meet her destiny among her own people and show no weakness.

But which bowl?

Slowly, so slowly, her hands crept forward. All the bowls looked alike. All the bowls smelled alike. One bowl was safe. Five bowls were death. *Which bowl was safe?*

And then a strange thing happened. The figure of her mother rose up in Shiva's mind. It was strange, for Shiva had never known her mother, who had died giving her life. But in her childhood years, Shiva had made pictures in her head, and those pictures, often as not, were of a handsome woman she called "Mother." Often she imagined that this handsome woman talked with her as mothers talk to daughters. Often, in her loneliness, she imagined this woman spoke of love.

Not that one! whispered the figure of her mother in her mind.

Shiva's hands moved away from the cup she might have chosen, moved toward another.

Not that one! the voice of her mother whispered again. *Take the cup at the end. Only that cup.*

Could she trust the voice? Sometimes the figures she imagined—her mother, a strong brown-haired man she thought of as her father and two girls she pretended were her sisters—warned her of dangers. And sometimes the dangers were real. Yet whatever she called them, these people were only pictures in her mind, creatures she created to ward off loneliness. Could she trust the voice? Her life depended on it.

She reached out and touched the bowl at the end. She heard a gasp from the surrounding crowd, but the Crone's features betrayed nothing.

"Drink!" the Crone ordered.

She had made her choice. One bowl was as good as any other. A curious calm poured over her, and Shiva took the bowl and drank. The draft was oily and intensely bitter. It burned her throat and churned her stomach, leaving a foul aftertaste. She set down the bowl.

14

For an eternity there was silence and stillness. Then, without warning, her breath caught in her throat. She reached forward to steady herself on the table, but her arm would not respond. She felt her knees buckle, heard a ringing in her ears.

There was a sudden eruption of excited chatter among the watching women as she teetered. Breath rasping, limbs convulsing, Shiva pitched forward into darkness.

2

Hiram's Hurt

Hiram squatted on a high rock, patiently chipping out an axehead for the hunt. His perch was a little distant from the camp, a granite pile arising out of the foothills like a giant's fist. From his vantage point he could see for miles now that the early-morning mist was lifting. The view, to him, was worth the chill discomfort and the difficulties of climbing the ice-covered rocks.

Immediately behind him, curving west northwest, was the run of the dark mountain range. Beyond it, he knew, lay the trails to the southlands and a more temperate winter with sufficient game.

But those trails were no more than a longing now, for the seven passes were each blocked by snow. They had been blocked for fifteen days.

Some members of the tribe had railed against Mamar, God of Ice, for coming early this year. But Hiram was more philosophical. If snow came early, snow came early. Shaking one's fist northward and abusing Mamar changed nothing. Indeed, he half suspected it might make the chill god more irritable than he was already, increasing the danger of hailstorms and blizzards.

Before Hiram was the plain where the great herds had grazed in summer. The hunting had been easy then, with much choice of meat from bison, ibex, chamois, aurochs and even mammoth. Almost all were gone now, migrated across the river, leaving only a sparse population of reindeer for food, supplemented by roots, berries, grubs, the occasional find of bird's eggs or a solitary badger.

Even river fishing was no longer possible. The river was flooded from recent rains, its few crossing points drowned and impassable. Anyone entering that flow—to cross it or to harpoon fish—would be swept away in seconds.

So the tribe was trapped. Hiram took that philosophically as well. He was young. He was strong. He would survive, and the experience might even sharpen his hunting skills. Besides, there was no alternative. Some said that to the

17

north and west a forest valley cut through the mountain chain, with open trails the whole year round. But that was only rumor, for there were ogres in the forest and no one ventured there who wished to live. No one, that was, but Shiva.

Hiram was in love with Shiva. He had first recognized the fact a little more than eighteen moons before, and since his feelings remained strong even now, he knew his love had to be real. He also knew he wanted to marry Shiva. Not yet, perhaps, but soon, in a year or two.

The trouble was, Hiram was not exactly sure that Shiva was in love with him. Certainly she did not want to marry him or anybody else just yet. She was a strange girl, solitary and inward. Most of the time it was impossible to tell what she was thinking. She saw the world differently from anyone he had ever known. That was one reason why he loved her. She had taught him to see certain things differently as well: the beauty in a sunset or a budding flower. He even found himself looking at animals differently, not simply as sources of food but as creatures made by the Mother and hence worthy of respect.

But he did not see everything as Shiva saw it. He was still afraid of ogres.

Even now he could remember the horror of

that distant day when ogres had captured him, carried him screaming to their forest lair and there prepared to eat his brains. Who could look on such as these with anything but horror? Not Hiram. Not any other hunter of the tribe. Yet the plain fact was that Shiva could.

Many of the Shingu still thought of Shiva as the child who had found the magic totem skull of Saber, the great cat of the dreamtime. This was natural enough, for the skull had brought fame and wealth to the tribe. But for Hiram Shiva was the girl who talked to ogres. The monsters actually liked her. Hiram shuddered. All the same, Shiva was easy to like. Hiram had liked her long before he had loved her.

Suddenly there was a movement below him.

The plain to the north was still free of snow, but here in the foothills there had been a light fall in the night. The movement below was no more than a flicker, white on white, but with his fine-honed hunter's instinct Hiram was certain something was down there. His guess would be a snow leopard.

He ceased his chipping and moved position. He was wary, but not particularly concerned. Even the largest of the leopards seldom tackled human prey. Besides, he had his spears. They had served him well, those spears. They would certainly protect him from a leopard now.

It was climbing toward him. Hiram stood up and gathered his spears. He pounded the haft on the ground to alert the creature to his presence. Often this was all that was needed to frighten off a leopard that crept too close to a man. Then it occurred to him that this cat must be aware of him. He had been making enough noise already as he chipped the flint axehead; and for certain the wind would have carried his scent.

The thought made Hiram uneasy. He looked around. The flat top of the rock was exposed and featureless, with a sheer drop on the northern side. He would be better off climbing down before the creature reached him.

He dropped the half-finished axehead into the rough skin pouch slung around his waist and gripped the crossed shafts of both spears in his right hand. Cautiously he glanced down, but there was no sign of any movement in the tangle of rocks below. He lowered himself, slid, then dropped, landing lightly, knees bent. He slid between two rocks and found the trail downward.

His first instinct had been correct. It was a snow leopard, but the beast had a starved look, its coat tufted and staring. He saw at once why it

20

had been stalking him. Part of one foreleg had been completely amputated, the stump ending in a raw and oozing wound.

The leopard snarled.

Hiram shifted one spear to his left hand and hefted the other to shoulder height in his right. He had no quarrel with the leopard, but the beast was obviously desperate enough to try to take him down.

Still snarling, the leopard hobbled forward. With neither fear nor malice, Hiram hurled the spear. An unthinking hunter's habit switched the second spear to his right hand, but he saw at once it was not needed. His throw had caught the leopard in the throat, penetrating deeply. The beast leaped back on itself, clawing feebly at the shaft, then rolled once and was still. One open eye stared up at Hiram in what might have been an expression of gratitude.

He moved forward to retrieve his spear. As he reached for the haft, the leopard's good forepaw lashed out and caught him on the shoulder. Hiram hurled himself backward, jabbing with the second spear. But it had been no more than a spasm. The cat was dead.

He could feel the warm ooze of blood beneath his heavy furs. Cautiously he pulled the skins away and discovered the cat had raked him on the upper arm. Fortunately the wound was not deep, although it bled profusely. He would have to ask one of the women to bind the wound with cleansing herbs.

The thought made him more nervous than the leopard had. Of all the things that Hiram feared, he feared women most of all. But there was no help for it. If he wished his wound dressed, only the tribeswomen had the skill. A hunter might bandage a wound to stop the blood, but he would have no skill at all with herbs. Only women learned that lore. Thus Hiram must control his fear of women—unless perhaps Shiva would treat his wound.

The thought cheered him mightily. Shiva had always been a sober child, almost frighteningly competent in everything she did. She had learned much about plants—this Hiram knew already—and while he had never actually seen her practice healing, he was sure she must know much about herbs as well. Besides, it would provide a ready excuse to talk with her, and if she could not help him, then he would be no worse off than he was before. He could simply find one of the older women, take his courage in his hands and request she minister to his arm.

With his furs pulled away, the biting cold had already dulled the pain. And as always when he suffered any injury, the bleeding had stopped quickly. He drew his spear from the body of the cat, wiped it clean of blood on his leggings and re-covered his wound.

For a moment he wondered if he should butcher the leopard, but decided against it. The creature was little more than skin and bones, scarcely worth eating even if a man were starving. The pelt was poor: little protection from the cold and no trophy. Besides, the missing foreleg meant the cat was incomplete, and that was bad luck for anyone who disturbed the body. The spirit of the leopard would even now be searching for its missing limb. Hiram wanted nothing to do with spirits.

He trotted off briskly in order to keep warm, since he had already lost some body heat while chipping at the axehead. In this season warmth was almost everything. If one lost too much of it, one grew sleepy and died. So Hiram trotted when there was no need for haste, and soon he was entering the village camp.

Wherever the tribe stopped on its seasonal migrations, the camp was always made in the same pattern. First there was raised the house of

23

women, a large communal structure where the old women and the young unmarried women and the children slept. Then came the house of men for the hunters. Next there was the long-house, where the Council of Elders held their deliberations and men and women came for acts of judgment. Finally, the tribe would raise the individual yurts: the hut of the chief, the hut of the Keeper of the Sacred Drums, the huts of the various married couples, each responsible for building their own shelter, and the lodge of the Crone.

Hiram skirted the lodge of the Crone, as most did who had no pressing business with her. The hut itself looked sinister. All other shelters were made from animal skins lashed to wooden poles. These were carried from site to site, frequently repaired and patched, erected as cones and held in place by local stones. But the lodge of the Crone was different. It was a dome-shaped structure of closely packed mammoth bones, anchored in a ring of mammoth skulls. Smoked hides of great black bear, the totem animal of the Crone, were stretched across the skeleton and clamped with mammoth jaws to prevent their tearing in the wind.

There was no hearth by the opening. Despite her age and the lack of fat on her wiry frame, the

Crone did not appear to feel the cold. There were some who whispered that she had once mated with Mamar himself and so was immune to his chill breath. Hiram was not certain he believed this, although he had no doubt at all that the Crone was able to ignore hardships in a way others of the tribe could not.

Not everyone slept in a yurt, of course, except in the very depths of winter when the shelters were buried in packed snow and very warm. At other times, there were always those who preferred the shelter of rock overhangs or trees, or perhaps just makeshift coverings of skins, provided a ringfire was nearby for warmth. Shiva was one of these. She had once told him she felt too restricted in a hut and the hearth smoke stung her eyes. When she could, she made her bed outside.

Hiram knew her favored sleeping spots, but quickly discovered she was not at any of them. He felt no surprise. Shiva was an early riser. At other sites she might have wandered from the camp itself. It was a habit that met with disapproval from her elders but was never broken. At this site, with winter having come early, it was unlikely she was too far away.

There was considerable activity to the south of

the camp as the men prepared their weapons for the morning hunt. Hiram glanced toward them. He planned to join the hunt as soon as his wound was dressed. Where was Shiva? He turned and almost walked directly into Elder Looca.

"Your pardon, Elder," Hiram muttered. He moved to get away from her.

But Looca, who knew him well enough, peered at him shortsightedly and said, "It's Hiram, isn't it? What are you doing here, boy? Why aren't you preparing for the hunt?"

She was the oldest of elders, but he disliked the way she called him *boy*. He swallowed his irritation and said politely, "I was looking for Shiva, Lady." He hoped she would not ask why he was looking for Shiva. The last thing he wanted was Elder Looca volunteering to dress his wound.

But she did not ask. For a moment she did not even speak. And from her expression Hiram knew on the instant something was dreadfully, horribly wrong. "Shiva?" he whispered, terrified to hear the answer.

Looca's head went back, her face set like a granite carving. "Shiva is no longer with us." Her nostrils flared at the scent of his fear, and he saw her wrinkled features soften. "I'm sorry, Hiram," she said, almost kindly.

3

Ogre Challenge

Was there ever, Hana thought, anything so stupid as a *man*? The women of the clan had always squabbled from time to time, particularly young women who might have their eyes on the same mate. But a squabble was a squabble, no big thing. Names were called. In a very bad case, hair might be pulled. But it never went further. It never got as bad as this. Only *men* could make a situation as bad as this.

She was squatting just inside the entrance to one of the highest caves, overlooking the clearing in the forest. The clearing was ringed by members of the clan, men and women but mainly men. There were children watching too, as children always did when something was forbidden. They lurked in the gloom of the cave mouths, and a few of the braver souls crept out to hide in bushes. All eyes were on the two men facing one another in the clearing.

Thag was almost directly below her, even greater in bulk today than when she had married him; although she had to admit that some of it was fat. They were growing old, both of them, but so gradually she had scarcely noticed until now. But all of a sudden she could see how gray his hair had become, how he moved more slowly than he once had.

Oh, he was still strong. The other night, stretched out in the smoky firelight of their deep cave, she had watched him absently crack the thigh bone of an auroch with his teeth. And only a few weeks before, Heft the Hunter had described to her how Thag had stunned a buffalo with one blow of his club. But was he still the strongest in the clan? It was a question that would be answered soon.

Facing Thag, squatted at the far side of the clearing, was Shil flanked by two of his cronies, Led and Metrak. They were talking loudly and excitedly together with extravagant gestures, preening and prancing and strutting before the crowd. Of the three, only Shil was important. Only Shil was strong enough to challenge Thag.

She stared across at Shil now, her nose wrinkling with disdain. He was not quite as broad as Thag, but he was certainly taller by two thumb breadths or more. His arms were longer too: not much, but perhaps enough to make a difference. And while, like Thag, he was turning gray, he was not so gray.

Thag was waiting with unaccustomed patience. Hagar stood by his shoulder, whispering something in his ear. Both looked unconcerned by what was about to happen, although that might be only show. Hana was certainly concerned. Twice before, Shil had challenged Thag for leadership of the clan. Twice before, Thag had sent him off bloody, bruised, battered and disappointed.

Would it happen again? Was Thag still the strongest of the clan?

In the middle of the clearing lay two clubs, heavy wooden bludgeons cut, shaped and polished just for these occasions. Each had a short strip of wolfskin tied loosely to the haft. No one knew why the wolfskin was there. It would be removed before the fight began, but it was tradition.

Those clubs could kill. Neither chief nor challenger was supposed to strike at the head, but even so, those clubs could kill. One blow could smash a ribcage, driving bone splinters into the heart. A broken arm could mean a slow death if it became infected. And a broken leg could leave a man crippled and useless even if it did not kill him.

Pictures were forming in Hana's mind, pictures of her mate, Thag, chief of the clan. In these pictures his gray hair was stained with blood.

What was wrong with men that they insisted on such sports? What was wrong with them that they bickered and maneuvered continually for position? What was wrong with them that they had to fight for leadership? If women ruled, there would be no such fights. They would simply decide among themselves who should lead (if, indeed, they ever needed a leader at all). If there was disagreement—unlikely but not quite impossible—they would vote, and she who got the most votes would be leader. It would be simple and so easy to avoid bloodshed and death.

But would the men adopt so sensible a system? Of course not! Men lived only to fight. They would fight over any prize or given any excuse. Two men would fight soon, one of them her mate.

There had been a time when fights excited her: fist fights and wrestling bouts between the young men to show off their strength and skill. She had first seen Thag in such a fight, facing not one opponent but two. Or rather, holding one opponent immobile in a red-faced stranglehold while he pounded at the other with his massive fist. What a magnificent brute he had seemed then! She had longed for him to notice her. But she had been young and foolish in those days, not knowing how a taste for fighting could rule a man.

Not that she regretted their mating, not for an instant. Thag had been a good mate, and chief of the clan. Best of all, they had created Doban together, a son now as strong and vigorous as his father had been in his prime.

No, Thag was her man, her love, brainless though he might be. And now something deep within her told her Thag faced special danger.

Below, Thag stood up and began to pace, stiff legged, back and forth. Hagar slipped away to hold a whispered conversation with Shil and his two companions. There was an immediate hum among the watching crowd.

The conference lasted longer than these things usually did, and at one point Hagar actually raised his voice, although Hana was too far to hear what he was saying. All four gesticulated angrily for a moment; then Shil's two compan-

31

ions broke away, leaving him alone. He too stood and stretched in an exaggerated sign of boredom. He stared upward, his eyes searching the higher terraces of the forest. He glanced downward at his feet. He looked casually over his left shoulder, then his right. At length he stared across at Thag. "Pebblehead!" he called.

"Dung eater!" Thag called back, almost calmly.

Both were deadly insults, but they generated little heat, for both were mere formalities at this place and time. Thag and Shil were here for a purpose, and both knew what that purpose was. The challenge had been issued, the challenge for the leadership of the clan. Soon the bloody battle would decide the outcome. Until then, all else was just a game. She saw Hagar melt into the crowd. It was almost time.

What if Thag should lose? He must lose someday. She knew that as certainly as she knew the sun must rise. If not today, then tomorrow or the next day or the day after that. Sooner or later a young bull would challenge him and overthrow him and become chief. It was in the nature of things. Already Thag had been clan chief far longer than any chief anyone could remember.

But was it bad if he ceased to be chief? As long as Thag was not killed or badly injured, it would not be so bad. No longer chief, he would still be honored by the clan. As former chief he would be brought meat when he grew too old to hunt. He would always be warm and well cared for. They would always be together. And if he craved action, he could teach his fighting skills to Doban, who might himself become a chief someday.

Perhaps she would have felt better had the challenger been anyone but Shil. Shil was not a young bull anymore. He was a man almost as old as Thag himself, a schemer with ambition. Some said he was a thief. Once, years ago, he had been accused of stealing Heft's meat and even brought to trial on the charge. But the trial was a farce as the men's trials always were, a matter of threats and growls and huffing and puffing. She had halted it herself, knowing Thag, the judge, had more important things to do. That was the time their Doban had been captured by the Weakling Strangers. Had she not insisted Thag take action, he might be with the Strangers yet.

She mistrusted Shil. No one would make as good a chief as her Thag (especially not when she stood behind his most important decisions), but Shil would make a bad leader. He thought too much of himself and too little of the clan. He was devious. He bullied to get his own way when he could and fawned when he could not. He lacked respect for tradition. All in all, he would make a poor leader.

Shil strode across the clearing, ignoring the clubs, and poked Thag in the chest. "Hogface!" he said loudly.

Thag made a backhanded swipe that caught him on the ear. Shil, who had obviously not been expecting so physical an insult just yet, staggered back a pace or two. Thag grinned. "Go home to your ugly mate," he said. "You are a bladder of wind and night soil."

The insults would be traded for some time now, growing worse until they led eventually to light blows. At that point the real contest would begin. Hana shifted her position, wondering why she felt so nervous. After all, Thag had fought often and always won. More important, he was seldom seriously injured. He was a big man, fast and strong. But was he still the strongest of the clan?

She turned at a small noise behind her and saw Hagar enter the cave from the warren of galleries and passages below. He too was looking old, his toothless mouth wrinkled and caving, his hair not simply gray but white.

He moved to her side, squatted and looked out across the clearing. Below them, Thag and Shil circled one another like stags. "This is bad business," Hagar whispered.

"These disputes are always bad business," Hana told him. Then, echoing an earlier thought she added, "Women would do it differently."

"Women have more sense," Hagar remarked, much to her surprise. He moved his hands in the darting motion that had always told her he was nervous. "But this dispute is worse than most. Shil has no love of tradition."

She waited, knowing he would tell her eventually, as he had always told her eventually since they were children together. To the clan and Thag, Hagar was the old wise man who gave counsel to the chief. To Hana, he was her brother.

"If he wins, he will banish Thag," Hagar said.

Hana chilled to the depths of her being. She swung around to stare directly at Hagar. "Banish?" she echoed. "He cannot banish Thag!"

Hagar shrugged sullenly. "If he wins, he will be chief; and the chief can do anything he wants. Who is there to stop him? Fortunately he will not win."

Five years ago Hana would have believed him. Even one year ago perhaps. Now she was not so sure. But she kept her worries to herself and said only, "How do you know he would banish Thag?"

"He told me to my face," Hagar muttered. "He told me thinking I would tell Thag and thus unsettle him."

"Did you? Tell Thag?"

Hagar shook his head. "No."

From below, Thag's voice floated upward in his own time-honored challenge. "I am strong! I am the strongest of the clan!" He made a small darting rush toward Shil, who fell back.

Banishment? It had never happened to a chief in living memory, although the storytellers of the clan taught that it had happened in distant times to a chief so evil that, once he was overthrown, the clan could no longer abide his presence. Did the clan feel that way toward her Thag? It was impossible. She felt a surge of fierce anger toward Shil for even thinking such a thing.

"It is against tradition, Hagar."

"Of course it is!" Hagar exploded with unaccustomed ire. "That's what I've just been telling you!"

It would be difficult to survive banishment in this season. It was winter, and even in the forest game was scarce. Soon there would be snow and even greater cold. The clan would retreat into the deep caves, which, while never warm, were never frozen either. Underground streams still flowed, while those on the surface turned to solid ice. There were blind fish to catch in the underground streams if food became scarce. Even the Weakling Strangers with all their magic buried themselves beneath the snow in the depths of winter—those few who did not run south from the cold. Was it possible for a man without his clan to live, however strong that man might be? She had faith in Thag. He was strong; he was stubborn and an excellent hunter. All the same, she could not be sure.

"It's starting," Hagar whispered.

They were walking toward the clubs. Those watching on the ground began to jump about and shout encouragement.

Chief Thag stood back disdainfully as Shil decided which of the two clubs he preferred. He made a great play of this, sniffing each, lifting each, waving each and finally picking one. He threw the other rudely to the ground beside Thag's feet.

"Thag will teach him a lesson in manners," Hagar murmured. He glanced at Hana, and something in her face prompted him to add, "He always has."

Thag picked up the second club and once again waited as Shil carefully removed the wolfskin strip from his own weapon. "I will peel your skin off like this wolfskin," he told Thag.

"Wind and night soil," Thag snarled back. He had a limited imagination for creative insults.

There were howls and catcalls from the crowd, mainly directed at Shil as far as she could judge. Not that it mattered. The only thing that mattered was who won the fight, no matter how he won. It was the tradition.

Thag turned his back on Shil and began to remove his strip of wolfskin with studied insolence. Shil promptly smashed his club into the back of Thag's thick neck, at the base of the skull. Thag pitched forward onto the hard, half-frozen ground. A pool of blood began to form around his head.

For an instant there was utter silence; then the clan erupted in uproar. Fists raised and shook. Insults were hurled. Some even threw back their heads and howled like wolves in anger and frustration. "Cheat!" Hana screamed, scrambling to her feet. "Foul hit!" Had she been below, on the ground, she would have hurled herself on Shil in her fury.

Shil ignored the uproar. He stepped across to where Thag lay and placed one broad foot on the bloodied head. His chest swelled. His head went back. "I have laid low the old chief!" he called loudly. "I, Shil, shall—"

Thag twisted, turned and snapped. His huge teeth closed on Shil's big toe. Shil screamed like a strangled rabbit. There was a horrid crunch.

"I shall kill you, Thag!" Shil roared. He smashed down with his club, clearly aiming at the head.

The watchers erupted in such violent booing that they sounded like an auroch herd. Thag shifted to one side, so that the blow grazed his ear but otherwise missed. From a sitting position he swung his own club (still adorned with its wolf-skin) and caught Shil on the knee. Shil staggered back and almost fell. Thag climbed back to his feet amid the delighted howls and cheering of the clan. He looked fit, despite the foul blow, but Hana thought his movements seemed unsteady, and certainly much of his agility had gone.

Shil hobbled forward and swung another vicious blow—to the body this time. Thag's club came up and blocked it. Shil swung again and missed. As he wound up for another swing, Thag pushed the club head into his stomach, and Shil doubled with a whoosh of air.

Hana waited for the inevitable follow-up—a lightning fast blow to Shil's exposed shoulders and upper back. But it never came. Thag stood swaying, watching his opponent.

Shil recovered and rushed at Thag again, head down, club circling, snorting like a rhino charging. Thag stepped to one side and suffered no more than a glancing blow to his right arm. He swung at Shil but, to Hana's surprise, missed completely.

"He has not recovered from the foul blow," Hagar whispered.

And indeed it was true. Thag stood, still swaying slightly, as Shil turned and rushed him again from the opposite direction.

"Look out, Thag!" Hana screamed.

Shil's club caught him at the base of the spine, propelling him forward. Thag turned and swung, landing a direct blow on his opponent's shoulder. Normally it would have paralyzed Shil's arm, but now it scarcely seemed to affect him at all. He brought his club around and struck Thag across the bridge of his flat nose.

This blow was definitely a foul, direct, deliberate hit to the head, against all rules of challenge conflict. The watching clan went half mad with anger, shrieking, screaming, hurling abuse. One or two small missiles sailed into the clearing in Shil's general direction.

But Hana made no sound at all. Her eyes, large and round, were on Thag as he crumpled, teetered, then fell like a forest tree. His club rolled from his nerveless fingers. He lay still. The crowd was suddenly silent.

Shil approached him far more warily this time, prodding at the supine body with his club, then finally giving it a sharp kick with his good foot. He turned, allowing his eyes to sweep around those watching. For an instant time stood still; then Shil growled, "I am Shil. I am strong. I am the strongest of the clan."

4

The Crone Speaks

Shiva awoke in a strange half-light, flat, dim and with a distinctly bluish tinge. Her head felt twice its normal size and pained her like an open wound. There was a dry, bitter taste in her mouth. When she moved, her entire body trembled. There was a narrow strip of black bearskin tied around her upper arm, outside the wrappings and the furs. Despite those same wrappings and furs, she felt cold as a corpse.

Cautiously she looked around. She seemed to be in a gloomy cavern, its contours picked out by a dim illumination that filtered through an opening in the roof high above her head. Although the floor was rock, and rubble strewn, the walls seemed to be made of ice, or at least covered by ice.

Behind her, deeper in the cave, a forest of slim ice pillars joined floor to roof. On her right was a frozen waterfall, locked in time. She found herself staring at it in something close to awe. It was the most beautiful thing she had ever seen.

Was this death?

The old women of the tribe had told her that on death, a woman's spirit flew to the dreamtime and was there gathered in the arms of the Mother. Shiva, who had never known her own mother, sometimes thought it might almost be worth the pain of death to experience the embrace of the Mother Goddess.

But while everyone knew about the dreamtime, everyone also knew that the ancestors dwelled in the deep caves and communicated with the Crone. So if the ancestors were gathered to the Mother on their death, they did not remain with her forever. At some time they came to the deep caves.

She had not thought much about death before, but then she had never faced the Ordeal by Poison before. She had no doubt now that she had chosen the wrong bowl. The Crone's poison had killed her, and perhaps she had gone directly to the deep caves. She wondered why. Had the Mother refused to meet her?

She found herself reviewing her life, searching for the sins that would have turned the Mother's face away from her. Was it the discovery of the skull of Saber that had angered her? The cat was, after all, the Mother's enemy, a creature banned from the dreamtime and thrown to earth on account of his arrogance and dishonesty. Shiva had found his skull by accident, falling into his ancient lair while fleeing from a rhino. Nobody could blame her for an accident, so nobody could blame her for the find. But perhaps the Mother was angry she had brought the skull back to her tribe.

Shiva sat up slowly, fighting both the pain in her head and the sudden nausea that welled up from her stomach. For a moment she thought she must vomit, but she did not. The sensations of sickness intrigued her. There was no illness in the dreamtime, no injury among the ancestors. Perhaps she was not dead after all.

She shivered. She still wore the furs, leggings and skin boots she had worn for sleeping, but even so she felt chilled to the bone. Her breath fogged before her like a smoke plume as she climbed painfully to her feet. Instinctively she checked for the flint knife strapped to her leg. It was not there! She could not have lost it, so it must have been taken. She had no knife, no axe, no spear, no club, no weapon of any sort. Wherever she was, she was defenseless, helpless.

Never helpless, hissed a dry voice from the gloom behind her, so softly it might have been her imagination.

Shiva turned so quickly that her head swam and her stomach heaved. She stood swaying for a moment, clutching desperately at consciousness. Then the sensations died and were replaced by a burgeoning excitement tinged with fear. She knew that voice!

"Lady Witch," she whispered. "Is that you?"

There was a dark, still shape among the forest of ice pillars, but so long as it remained unmoving, Shiva could not be sure it was the Crone. She strained her eyes, then moved forward to see.

Stop! the Crone's voice ordered.

Shiva stopped. Confusion washed over her like a wave.

You have survived the Ordeal by Poison, the Crone informed her softly.

So she was not dead. Somehow she had selected the one bowl without the poison, although it had obviously contained the juices of a sleeping plant. Since she was not dead, where had they taken her?

You will find that out soon enough, the Crone said. *For now, stay calm and listen.*

Was it the Crone? Shiva craned forward but still failed to make out features in the dark shape. It might have been no more than a shadow in the gloom. The strange half light was horribly deceptive. "Lady Witch—"

Listen! hissed the Crone again, an edge of anger in her tone.

Shiva bit back her words and waited. For a long moment there was silence in the cave. The silence extended until Shiva became certain the Crone's voice had existed only in her mind. The shape among the icy pillars was only a shadow, a trick of this strange light. Perhaps she was still not free of the juices of the sleeping plant: Perhaps she dreamed.

No dream, the Crone's dry voice whispered. *Not a dream.*

"Why am I here, Lady Witch?" asked Shiva, unmindful of the order to be quiet.

There was another moment of silence, but shorter this time. Then the Crone's voice floated to her from a different corner of the cave. *You were always a strange child, Shiva.*

Shiva spun around and this time suffered neither dizziness nor nausea. It was not her imagination. The Crone was definitely here. But where? The witch moved at will from one part of the cave to another, without sound or any other indication. There was nothing in the corner from which her voice had come.

"Where are you, Lady?" Shiva called. But the question she really wished to ask was *Why do you call me a strange child?*

This time the voice seemed to emerge from somewhere deep within the frozen waterfall. *Your mother died giving birth to you,* the Crone said, *yet you have spoken to her often.*

The Crone knew! The Crone knew how she made pictures of her mother in her mind. But how? She had told no one of this, not even Hiram.

There are few in the tribes who can create such pictures, the Crone's voice murmured. *And none among the Shingu who can create them with such skill as you.*

"You can, Lady Witch!" Shiva protested. Everyone knew the Crone created pictures in her mind and made great magic with them when she painted in the deep caves.

Ah yes, the Crone said, *so I can. And that is why you are here.*

For some reason a thrill of fear trickled along

47

Shiva's spine. This time she said nothing, the sudden terror clamping her tongue like a tiger's jaws.

I want you for my own, the Crone said baldly.

Thoughts began to tumble through Shiva's mind like pebbles poured from a pouch. "What do you mean, Lady?"

I want you for my own, the Crone repeated. *You will be the next Crone of the Shingu tribes. That is why I have marked you with the bearskin band.*

It was like a thunderclap inside her head. For a long moment she was still and calm; then, with a deliberation all of its own, her body began to shake. She found herself watching it as if she had somehow moved outside herself. Shivers chased along her arms, her legs. Her hands fluttered like leaves in a breeze. Her mouth formed words but stammered. "Ah—Crone of the Sh-Sh-Shingu tribe? Lady, I—"

Spare me, sighed the Crone. *You are too young. You are afraid. You do not want it.*

Suddenly, Shiva knew where the Crone was. To the left of the frozen falls, there was a natural niche cut deep into the ice wall of the cavern. The Crone was there, squatting huddled, the black bearskin drawn around her. Even in the half-light Shiva saw the glittering of her eyes.

"I am too young," whispered Shiva. Involuntarily she fingered the strip of black bearskin tied around her upper arm. "Please, Lady Witch, I am afraid. I don't want to be a Crone!" Nor did she. Magic frightened her, and a Crone's whole world was magic. A Crone conversed with spirits of the dead. A Crone painted the mystic pictures in the deep caves to bring success to the hunt. A Crone looked to the past and future, interpreting the destinies of people and of tribes. A Crone was Guardian of the Sacred Totems. A Crone protected her people and laid curses on their enemies. A Crone was feared and walked alone.

"Listen well," the Crone said, her voice much stronger now that Shiva had located her position. "Nineteen moons ago, I became Hag to all the tribes. The Crones chose me as Crone of Crones because they knew my skills and knew my dedication to my tribe, the Shingu. I shall not pretend their trust has been misplaced. I am what I am. Yet in one respect I have long failed the Shingu. I am no longer young, have not been young for many, many years. Yet never have I sought to train a new Crone to take my place."

There was a rustle from the niche as if the Crone were shredding dried herbs or withered leaves.

Shiva said, "Lady Witch, you could not know you would be called to be the Hag!"

"No," the Crone agreed. "But I have always known I would be called sometime to the Mother. All of us must die, Shiva. It is the duty of a Crone to ensure her skills and magic do not die with her." An audible sigh floated from the darkness of the niche. "I did not entirely neglect that duty, not entirely. I sought for one who might follow me. But to become a Crone is no simple matter. It is not like becoming a hunter, or even a tribal chieftain. A Crone needs certain skills and talents. The skills may be learned, but the talents—ah, the talents are inborn. I found none with the talents. Until—"

"Until?" asked Shiva, half to herself.

"Until you were five years old and I discovered you could make pictures in your mind."

Five years old? Ten years ago. Had the Crone been watching her for ten long years? It seemed almost unimaginable, yet who could say what a Crone might do?

The Crone was continuing to speak. "Of course, pictures in the mind are only one small part of it. But I watched and I waited and hoped the ancestors would send me a sign. I saw you had courage, Shiva. I saw you were resourceful far beyond your years. These things were important, but still I waited. Once, without guidance, you managed to discover the Ring of Stones, which only Crones may know. I thought that might be the sign I sought, yet I could not be sure. So I waited still. And then you found the skull of Saber and I knew I had my sign. I knew the ancestors had marked you clearly as the one who was to follow me."

"Lady Witch," said Shiva, more in confusion than in anger, "you tried to poison me."

"No woman may become a Crone without passing through the Ordeal, for only the spirits of the ancestors can guide her hand to the right bowl. You have survived the Ordeal, Shiva, as I survived it once, long, long ago. Now there is another test."

"Another test?" Shiva echoed.

"A test of courage and endurance. A test of strength, intelligence and skill. A test of intuition. A test of the love the Mother bears for you. A test of the way that fortune smiles on you. A test of your destiny. It has many aspects, but in essence it is simple enough."

It was almost too much for her to comprehend. She was to be Crone? It was impossible! She had no wish to be Crone, no wish to be anything other than what she was: a girl of the Shingu with no particular importance. Yet for all the terror that poured through her soul like the spring torrents, the Crone's words held her spellbound.

"You will test me, Lady?" Shiva asked hesitantly.

"Not I," the Crone said at once.

"Who then?"

"That you will find out when you leave this cavern."

She thought of the Ordeal by Poison and shuddered. But perhaps that was the worst. Perhaps the rest would be easier. And perhaps if she failed, she would not have to become a Crone.

"What happens if I fail?" she heard her tongue ask of its own accord.

There was a ringing silence in the cave. Then the Crone said quietly, "You die."

5

A Hunt Begins

Shiva was not dead! She could not be dead! The thought chased itself around and around in Hiram's mind, driven by a fear so intense it teetered on the edge of panic. *No longer with us,* Looca had said, an expression often used by the women when they meant someone had died. But when Hiram asked bluntly, *Is she dead?* the Elder would not look him in the eye and would not answer. She walked away. But Shiva could not be dead. Not Shiva. She was far too careful, far too skilful. Besides, the ancestors protected her: Had she not escaped the rhino and found Saber's skull?

The hunt had left without him now, but he did not care. All he had ever cared about was Shiva. Now she was gone. But where?

The women knew. He had seen it in their faces. The women knew, all right. But the men did not.

Hiram had run to Kendar, the leader of the hunt, and asked about Shiva. Kendar did not know. But Kendar smelled the fear in Hiram and asked the other hunters, men of the Shingu who knew Hiram well and liked him, who hunted with him and admired his skill. They knew, as everybody knew, that Hiram was in love with Shiva. These men, his comrades, wished him well and would have helped him if they could. But none, not one of them, knew anything at all of Shiva.

He asked the old men then, for the old men did not hunt and seldom moved far from the camp. They talked to one another, sometimes brooded, but more often watched while they waited for the Mother's call to the dreamtime. There was little that happened that they did not know. Yet the first group he asked did not know what had happened to Shiva, nor did the second.

But near the third group Hiram questioned was an old man named Mam, for Mamar, God of Ice, a toothless, undernourished creature whose digestion could no longer cope with meat. He was one most of the tribe avoided, partly because of the smell that wafted from his body, partly because he talked a great deal and would not let a listener go. Hiram was too desperate to avoid him.

"Shiva?" asked Mam, although there was nothing at all wrong with his hearing. "You are looking for Shiva, the girl who found our skull?" But then, when Hiram nodded eagerly, he did what he so often did and began to talk of something else entirely. "I can't sleep, you know. Not at all. Well, not often. And not at night. It happens when you're my age." He leaned forward so that his smelly old face was close to Hiram's own. "Do you know what age I am, young fella?"

Hiram backed away a step and tried to hold his breath. He shook his head.

"Neither do I," said Mam. "But I'm older than most. If you get to be my age, or even close, you won't sleep either. You don't need as much when you get older, and eventually you don't need any. Like me."

"Shiva, sir." Hiram prompted. He looked around him. There must be someone who knew.

"Yes, yes—the girl who found the skull. The one who caught the ogre cub. I'm not stupid, you know."

"No, sir, I'm sure you're not," Hiram agreed. "It's just that—"

But Mam was listening only to his own voice. "When you don't sleep, the nights get very long. I have my own place, you know, my own hut. They won't let me sleep in the house of men anymore. They say it's because I don't wash, but it's my belief that washing weakens a man. Stop washing now, young fella, and you'll live as long as me."

"Yes, I'll do that," Hiram promised, "but I was wondering—"

"When you have your own hut and don't sleep, there's nobody to talk to. Everybody else is asleep, except me, so there's nobody, not when they won't let you into the house of men. And I wouldn't go into the house of women, of course, not at my age." His eyes glazed slightly and he cackled like a crow.

"No, of course—"

"So when there's nobody to talk to, what do you do? I'll tell you, young fella: You talk to *yourself*!" He stopped like one who had just revealed something startling and important. A thin but surprisingly strong hand reached out to grip Hiram's wrist as Hiram moved to slip away. "I like to walk while I talk to myself, leastways at night. So often I walk out of my hut and around the camp. Look here. Look there. Sometimes you see things, sometimes you don't. Mostly you don't, because people hear you coming."

Hiram tried to pull his wrist away. "Sir, I—"

"Hold still, young fella. I saw something last night."

Hiram became immobile as a startled shrew.

"The women," Mam said. "They were up to something."

There was a tightness in Hiram's chest that made it difficult to breathe. "What?" he asked.

"I don't know," Mam said. "I don't see so well at a distance, and I wasn't risking getting too close or the women would have chased me back into my hut. But they were painted and they were up to something with that girl Shiva. I saw them take her out of the camp."

"They took her?"

"That's right." He sniffed and released Hiram's wrist. "But they didn't bring her back."

So women from the tribe had taken her. "Who was there?" he asked Mam.

Mam shrugged. "Women," he said vaguely. "The important ones."

Hiram left him then and went to squat between two rocks to think. His hands nervously scratched for grubs to eat, for fear always made him hungry. But the ground was hard, and any

57

insects were well hidden. He stared hungrily into the middle distance, thinking. Women had taken her from the camp but had not brought her back. The women knew what had happened, knew where she was. If he asked, would they tell him? He doubted it. Looca had not told him, although as an elder she must have known.

Who among the women took her? *The important ones,* Mam said. The older women, not the young girls who might have told Hiram what he wished to know. The older women would not tell him. They would never tell him. Unless—He was up and moving even as the thought occurred to him.

He found her scraping the skin of a small rodent she had killed. She looked up at his approach, and something in her face told him she knew what he was about. But she said only, "Not gone with the hunt, Hiram?"

He shook his head. "No, Mother." She did not sit on the elder council, but she was Keeper of the Sacred Drums, an important member of the tribe. She must know what they had done to Shiva. She stared at him soberly, waiting.

"Shiva," Hiram said.

Sheena, his mother, nodded. "Yes."

"They have taken her."

She nodded again. "Yes."

58

"Why?" Hiram exploded. "Why have they taken her? Where have they taken her? Is she dead?" He became a child again on the instant and ran in his misery to his mother and embraced her as he had not done for years.

Her arms went around him. "You're fond of Shiva, aren't you, Hiram?"

"I love her!" Hiram sobbed.

"Perhaps," Sheena said. "She is very young." As an afterthought, she added, "So are you."

"She isn't dead. She can't be dead!"

Sheena said nothing.

"Is she dead, Mother?" Hiram yelled.

"I don't know."

He broke away from her in something close to horror. What was happening? What had they done to Shiva? Why would no one tell him?

Sheena said, "We did not kill her. She was alive and well when we took her from the camp."

His eyes widened. "*We?* Were you with them?"

Sheena nodded. "Yes."

His hands worked convulsively. He wanted to seize her, shake her. But she was his mother. After a moment he gained a measure of control. "Where did you take her? Why did you take her?"

For a long moment Sheena stared at him. Then, with the air of one who has made a decision, she said, "Shiva is to be tested. That is all I can say."

"Where have you taken her?" he screamed.

"I'm sorry, Hiram, I can't tell you that. Only certain people know where she was led, and I am not one of them."

He ran from her then, ran from the camp and hid away among the rocks, nursing his panic and confusion. He had to find out where the women had taken Shiva. He had to know. Even if he never learned the reason, he had to find out where. Winter had come early. They were trapped north of the mountains. Anyone who left the tribe in this season was doomed to death. He had to find where they had taken her and bring her back.

There was one who would know.

The thought, as it occurred, brought its own special terror. But he fought the terror and dared to think the thought. There was one who would know. There was one who might tell. If he dared to ask.

He loved Shiva. He would dare anything.

Hiram walked back to the camp like one in a dream. He went directly to the lodge of the Crone. His footsteps slowed as he approached. There was no one near, neither men nor women.

A bearskin curtain hung across the entrance to the lodge, but there was no barrier, no guards, nothing to stop his sweeping it aside and stepping in.

He stopped. The dead eye sockets of the mammoth skulls stared balefully toward him. His heart was pounding in his chest. The spears in his left hand slid to the ground. Unarmed, he took a faltering step forward.

There was a muttering of voices from within the lodge. The Crone was not alone.

Hiram closed his eyes. He could not turn back now. He had to know where they had taken Shiva. His eyes flicked open. He moved forward, drew back the curtain and stepped inside.

For a moment he could make out little detail in the gloom of the lodge. Then his eyes adjusted. The Crone was seated no more than three yards away from him, her eyes wide, blank and staring. A tiny wood fire had died before her and the air was stale with the smell of burned narcotic herbs.

The Crone spoke. "A test of courage and endurance," she said in a hollow voice. "A test of strength, intelligence and skill. A test of intuition."

Hiram froze. Why did she speak to him thus? He had expected anger, or the chill, brutal gaze of the Crone while he explained the reason for his

61

intrusion. But not this. He remembered suddenly that his mother had spoken of a test for Shiva. Now the Crone talked of tests as well. "Lady Witch," he mumbled, "I—" He stopped. Her head had not turned toward him, her eyes had not moved. She was not aware of his presence.

"A test of the love the Mother bears for you. A test of the way that fortune smiles on you. A test of your destiny. It has many aspects, but in essence it is simple enough," the Crone said softly.

She did not even know that he was here. If he had been frightened before, he was terrified now. He had dared to enter her lodge while the Crone was working magic. He would die. His soul would wither. There was not another in the tribe who would dare to interrupt the Crone while magic was afoot.

"Your pardon, Lady," Hiram mumbled. "I did not know—" He started to back out from the lodge.

He had scarcely taken two paces when it happened. "You will test me, Lady?" Shiva's voice said clearly.

"Not I," the Crone replied at once.

Hiram spun, staring around the lodge. Dried plants hung from the roof. A small heap of twigs lay to one side. There was a pile of sleeping furs.

But apart from the Crone and himself, the lodge was empty. Yet he had definitely heard Shiva's voice!

"Who then?" asked Shiva's voice. He knew every lilt and intonation, knew from her tone that she was wary, frightened. It was Shiva's voice.

"That you will find out when you leave this cavern," said the Crone.

Why did she speak of a cavern? Hiram began to shiver. Women frightened him and magic frightened him. Women's magic frightened him most of all.

"What happens if I fail?" asked Shiva. And suddenly, in horror, Hiram saw. Shiva was speaking through the mouth of the Crone.

Hiram felt himself stagger as if he had been struck an actual blow. At the great ceremonies of the solstice and the equinox, he had watched in fearful fascination while the spirits of the ancestors took control of the body of the Crone. Now Shiva's spirit was within her too. Was Shiva dead?

The Crone said quietly, "You die."

She would not die if she was already dead. She could not be already dead. Something snapped like a twig inside Hiram's head, and suddenly his

63

fear was gone, suddenly there was only rage within him. "Where is she?" he screamed at the Crone.

"Where am I?" Shiva's voice asked, as if echoing Hiram's question.

"You are in Mamar's Kingdom," said the Crone.

6

Into Exile

The clan was very, very quiet. No one moved. No one jostled. No one complained. They surrounded the clearing, peered from the cave mouths, clung to the cliff face—men, women, children—and watched without a word.

There was a boulder in the center of the clearing, rolled there on the orders of Chief Shil, who now perched atop it, claiming it to be the Rock of Judgment. As if everyone did not know the real Rock of Judgment, hallowed by tradition, was in the deep caves, in the Cavern of Judgment, where it had been for generation upon generation.

Below the boulder, armed with clubs, were four of Shil's closest cronies: the inevitable Led and Metrak, Dag the Flint Chipper, and the repulsive Og-nar, who strutted and grinned and preened and threw his weight around now that Shil, at last, had come to power. All four carried clubs, although they did not go to hunt and the clan was not under threat. It was another change that Shil had instigated. He was calling them his guards.

Hana lay just inside the mouth of a ground-level cave, her arms tightly bound. Beside her, bound more heavily, wrists tied to ankles, was Doban, her son. Beside them was her brother Ha-gar, advisor to Thag. Shil had left him untied, claiming he represented no threat at his age, which was probably true. But it was also true that Hana represented no threat either, and that had not stopped Shil from issuing his orders. So the reason she was tied was not the reason Shil had given.

Was Thag dead? He had seemed dead when they had carried him back into the caves, his huge body limp and bleeding. She had wanted to minister to him, but Shil's men had caught and tied her for reasons of their own. Now she could only lie in this cave mouth and wait while her mate bled. She could see Shil on his rock-top perch, bouncing on his heels, eyes glittering with excitement. He had wanted to be Chief for many years. Now Chief he was, even though he had cheated in the fight.

"Bring him out!" Shil called, raising one arm grandly. She noticed he seemed to have developed many extravagant gestures since he had climbed onto his rock. But bring whom out? Perhaps it meant Thag was not yet dead. Or did Shil wish them to bring out the body?

"I go, great Chief," screamed Og-nar the Repulsive. He scampered past Hana into the warren of caverns riddling the cliff face.

"What are they doing?" Hana asked quietly of Hagar. She had stilled her tongue until now, not wishing to upset Doban, but could still it no longer.

Hagar moved instinctively into the shadows. "Og-nar goes for Thag," he whispered.

"I know Og-nar goes for Thag!" spat Hana angrily. "I'm not a fool! I want to know if you think he's still . . . ?" She let it trail, glancing at Doban, who was slumped, head bowed, staring at his feet.

"Only Og-nar went to fetch him," Hagar murmured.

For an instant she did not realize what he meant; then her stomach tightened in renewed fear. No man would ever go to fetch her Thag

67

alone, not if he valued his hide. Unless Og-nar planned to carry out a corpse.

She lay for an eternity, waiting, locked in a nightmare that was composed of fear and hope and sorrow in a mixture almost too painful to be borne. Hagar did not speak again. Doban said nothing. Outside, the clan had grown very still. Only Shil and his guards moved, Shil rocking on his heels, teeth bared, the guards pacing and scratching like restless cats with fleas.

There were sounds from the inner caves. Bound tightly as she was, Hana had to roll her entire body to see behind her. Even then it was difficult, for her eyes did not adjust at once to the gloom of the cavern. But then Og-nar appeared, dragging Thag. And while she knew at once he was not dead, she also knew why Og-nar had dared to go alone. Thag staggered and trembled like one far gone in sickness or who has eaten poisonous plants.

All the same, there was still a glint of anger in his eye. He stopped while still within the cavern, his lips curling as his gaze fell first on Hana then on Doban. "Shil has done this?" he breathed.

No one answered. Og-nar made to push him forward, but Thag, weak though he was, shook his hand away.

"Shil is chief now?" Thag asked loudly, glaring all about him.

"Yes," Hana told him shortly. Now that she knew for certain he was not dead, the relief that washed over her made her angry with him.

"He did not beat me fairly," Thag said. There was a look of something close to puzzlement in his brown eyes. "He hit me on the head."

"That's true, but he's still chief." It would take very little, she knew, to send Thag lurching at Shil, determined to renew the battle. If he did, he would surely die. His nose was a bloody mess. He had difficulty turning his head. One shoulder had swollen so much that his left arm hung almost useless. She suspected he might have a broken rib. He could not stand without swaying. Shil had been almost untouched. He would kill Thag in another fight.

She turned her head to look at Shil and noticed Thag's great friend, Heft the Hunter, stood near the cave mouth, face expressionless. There were many of Thag's friends in the watching crowd. They could do nothing. The fight had been lost. There was a new chief. That was the tradition.

Thag leaned heavily against the cavern wall. "Where is Hagar?" he demanded loudly, obviously having forgotten he was no longer chief.

But so, apparently, had Hagar. "Here, Thag," came the whispered voice. Hagar stepped from the shadows, looking grayer and more ancient than ever.

"Will you advise Shil?" Thag asked. He glared at Hagar. Perhaps he had not forgotten after all.

Hagar slowly shook his head. "I will not. The man can find his own advice."

"Will you advise me, even though I am no longer chief?"

"You are my sister's mate. I will advise you."

For a long moment Thag said nothing. He looked very tired, very ill and very old. Even before the fight he had spoken privately to Hana about giving up the chieftainship. Now, for the first time, she believed he might actually have done it. "What happens now, Hagar?" he asked at length.

"You must leave the clan," Hagar said almost brutally. "Shil, the chief, has ordered your exile."

"And not too soon!" Og-nar called out cheerfully. He had never had much status in the clan and was generally disliked for his stupidity and brutality. His change in fortune obviously delighted him.

"That is not the tradition," Thag growled, ignoring him.

"A chief can overrule the tradition," Hagar said. "You yourself—" He stopped, plainly deciding it was no time to remind Thag of the many times he had overruled tradition.

"Why does Shil break with tradition?" Thag asked. He looked directly at Hagar.

For a moment Hana thought Hagar would not answer. But the habits of years reasserted themselves. With obvious reluctance, he said softly, "He wants you dead."

And there it was, in a single, brutal phrase. Shil's decision to banish Thag was a sentence of death. That was clear enough. But the decision had all Shil's notorious low cunning. Obviously he had no stomach for a return fight with Thag, for while he might win now, later, when Thag's wounds had healed, could well prove a different story. In a return fight, Thag would know what to expect and would know how to protect himself against Shil's cheating. In such circumstances, older though he was, slower though he was, Thag might win. It was a possibility Shil was not prepared to risk. So if Thag did not die from the blow to the head, then he must be killed some other way.

But not outright, not obviously. There would be enough mutterings within the clan about the way Shil had cheated in the fight. Even as chief, he could not afford an accusation of murder. So he had ordered exile, knowing that in this season, with the first heavy snows only days away, a man with Thag's injuries could not possibly survive alone.

And suddenly Hana knew why she and Doban had been tied. They were no threat to anybody, whatever Shil might claim. But he had no wish that they should leave the clan with Thag. They might manage to keep him alive, or even to nurse him back to health.

Crouched behind Thag, listening to Hagar's chilling words, Og-nar chuckled.

"Is there anything to be done?" Hana asked, knowing the answer yet desperate. "Is there any way that Thag can stay?"

Hagar looked uncomfortable. "He might ask Shil to reconsider."

"That's it." Og-nar grinned. "Beg Shil for mercy, Thag! If you grovel, he might let you stay until the spring."

Thag's eyes flickered toward him and he growled deep in his throat. Hana noted with some satisfaction that Og-nar dropped back a pace. But it was a hollow victory. Thag was still breathing heavily, and despite the chill of the season, pain was pushing droplets of sweat out onto his brow.

Eventually he asked, "Who else is *Chief* Shil sending from the clan?"

"None other, Thag."

Thag turned and struck the wall of the cavern with his good hand. It was a feeble blow. He looked around him, the bewilderment creeping back into his dark eyes. Even Hana could say nothing to help him, nothing to ease his confusion and his pain. Eventually he said, "I leave the clan alone?"

"Where you go, I go," Hana said at once.

"Shil will not let you go," sneered Og-nar. "You stay here—you and the cub." He glanced at Doban, who still had not looked up.

"He is right," Hagar said.

Doban looked up suddenly. "I want to come with you. I will follow you when they release me."

"You are a child!" Hana snapped. He was, in fact, every inch as tall as his father now and almost as broad, but that made no difference, no difference at all. She often thought his father was a child as well, although she took care not to tell him so. "You are also a fool." Which was something she *had* said to his father; and frequently.

73

"The snows come soon. An hour, two hours, a day at most. Shil will not release you until it snows. Then you cannot track your father. You will die in the snows."

"She is right, Doban," Hagar said soberly.

By the entrance, Og-nar said, "You come now, Thag. Shil commands it."

Hagar stepped forward just in time to stop Thag launching himself shakily at the man's throat. Over his shoulder he said, "Thag comes now." He gripped Thag's upper arms and looked into his dark eyes. "You must leave now," he said softly, "for it is the tradition of the clan that the chief must be obeyed. You must leave now, for Shil is chief and Shil has ordered it and all must obey the chief."

"I will fight Shil again!" yelled Thag. "I will fight him again and win!" He tried to jerk away, but Hagar held him easily, another indication of his weakened condition.

Had Hana been free, she would have kicked him on the ankle, more gently than usual on account of his injuries, but sharply enough to catch his attention. As it was, she only shouted, "You are a fool, Thag! You were always a fool. In your youth you were a young fool and now you are an old fool, which is worse. You cannot fight Shil

74

again. You are injured. An injured man does not fight to become chief. An injured man fights to become dead."

"Why do you do that?" Thag asked. "Why do you call me fool? Why do you shout at me?"

Hana threw her eyes upward. They had been together many seasons. She sighed then muttered, "Because I love you!"

Thag stared at her. Hagar slid into his familiar position by the left shoulder. "Which is why you must go, Thag," he whispered. "Doban and Hana will stay."

Thag half turned toward him. "Shil will harm them!"

"Shil will not harm them. He fought to be chief, but a chief may not harm women and boys."

Doban, said, "I am not a b—" He stopped at a glance from Hagar, who said to Thag: "I shall protect them, I and Heft the Hunter."

Thag looked from his son to his mate, from his mate to his old advisor, from his old advisor outward to the waiting clan. His shoulders sagged. "I will go," he said shortly. He moved unsteadily toward the exit from the caves.

There was a murmur, like a rising of summer bees, as he emerged into the clearing. From her position in the cave mouth, Hana could clearly read the shock and pain on a hundred faces.

Shil jumped to his feet, voice high with excitement. "See?" he screamed. "See the great *chief*? Where are you now, Thag?" He leaned forward from his perch on the rock and taunted: "Who is the strongest of the clan now, Thag?"

"Aye," echoed Og-nar, grinning. "Who is the strongest of the clan now, Thag?"

For a moment Hana was certain Thag must attack, but he did not, merely stood swaying in front of Shil's Rock of Judgment.

"You have been beaten in a fair fight," Shil began, to a murmur from the crowd so angry that he was forced to wait until it had died down before continuing. "I am chief now, and my word is law." He looked around challengingly. None denied him. He turned back to stare down at Thag, his lips curled into a condescending sneer. "You were always a bad chief, Thag. A fool and a bully. Now you are chief no longer and my clan has no place for you. I am chief. I am judge. I sit on the new Rock of Judgment. I say you must leave!" He looked around. "What say you?" he called.

"He must leave!" his four cronies shouted dutifully. The remainder of the clan was silent.

Although he still seemed to be having trouble

76

standing upright, Thag said, "What if I do not leave?"

"I shall kill you!" Shil shouted.

Thag shrugged.

Shil leaned forward again. "And when I have killed you, Thag," he said, "I shall club your mate and club your son!"

There was a stunned silence that hung as palpable as fog. In the clearing, it began to snow gently, a small foreshadowing of the blizzards soon to come.

Thag's gaze dropped. "I go," he said simply, and so quietly that Hana could scarcely hear him. Og-nar fell in beside him as he slowly crossed the clearing. He reached the ring of clanspeople, and for just the briefest moment it appeared they might not let him go; then they broke apart to permit him through. Faces turned away from him in sorrow and in shame.

Still escorted by the leering Og-nar, Thag walked painfully toward the forest's edge. It was snowing harder now, and his hair and his furs were turning white. His arm still hung useless. He seemed to be breathing heavily in considerable pain. He stopped often, swaying.

At last he reached the trees. The great forest loomed over him, higher even than the cliff face.

Thag stopped and turned, a lonely figure, his eyes traveling slowly over the cave warren that had been his home for so long. Then he turned again and stepped into the forest.

As he did so, he used his uninjured arm to sideswipe Og-nar, who dropped his club and doubled up in agony.

7

In Mamar's Kingdom

They had carried her to Mamar's Kingdom. Shiva felt her body stiffen with fear. The Ice God's Kingdom was an empty wasteland, a region of snow and rock and ice so hostile that few people of the tribe had ever seen it, save from its boundaries, and lived.

She swallowed past the terror in her throat. "What is my test?"

"Only this," the Crone said gravely. "To embrace me, kiss me, take the totem pouch from around my neck and place it around your own. That only."

It seemed simple. A little frightening, for who in the tribe would dare to embrace and kiss the Crone, then take the totem pouch so filled with magic? Yet if this was the test, then the Crone must will it.

A fierce joy rose in Shiva's breast. She had survived the Ordeal by Poison. Now nothing more remained except this simple test. She would live.

"Lady Witch," she said eagerly, "I wish to take my test at once. May I approach you?"

There was no answer.

"Lady Witch, did you hear me?"

Still nothing. From the depths of the cavern, beyond the forest of frozen pillars, there was a single, sharp snapping sound, like ice cracking. Shiva scrambled to her feet. The test was obviously a test of her courage in the face of magic, for the totem bag was magic and would not be touched by any member of the tribe; and the Crone herself was magic, a woman everyone avoided unless there was need. Shiva moved toward the niche beside the waterfall where the witch was crouched.

The niche was empty. The Crone could not have moved from it, for Shiva was close by and would have seen her.

"Lady Witch," she whispered uncertainly.

Only a heavy silence answered, accentuated by a distant drip of water. She was alone.

"Lady Witch!" screamed Shiva, her voice echoing throughout the cave. "Where are you? Please help me, Lady Witch. Where are you?"

But the cavern was empty. Shiva turned away.

What now? How could she undergo the test when—? The question halted, half formed in her mind as realization dawned. The Crone had told no more than the truth. She was being tested. Tested for courage, endurance and much else, for to kiss the Crone and take the pouch, she must first discover where the witch was hiding. And a sudden intuition exploding in her thoughts told her that the Crone was not in the cavern and had never been in the cavern, however clearly Shiva heard her voice.

If not in the cavern, then where? Doubtless still with the tribe in her mammoth-skull lodge in the village camp pitched in the foothills. For Shiva to undertake the test, she must first find her way back from Mamar's Kingdom to the village of her people. Death was the penalty for failure.

And a much worse penalty for success, her mind whispered. If she survived, she would be Crone.

Even now the thought was unimaginable. The Crone was old; ancient beyond belief. How could Shiva be the Crone? And yet there were young Crones. At the last Star Jamboree she had seen the newly made Henka Crone, tiny, slight, dark eyed, smiling and scarcely more than seven years older than Shiva herself. And the Crone of the Tomara was the same age as Renka, the Shingu chief. Most Crones were old women, but not all.

Shiva's jaw set firmly. She would survive. It was as much a decision as a conviction. She would survive and find her way back to the tribe. And there she would accept whatever fate awaited her.

How difficult could survival be, even in Mamar's Kingdom? Life had never been easy. The tribe looked after its own so no one starved, but as an orphan child she had often gone hungry until she had learned what roots were good to eat and where to find supplies of grubs. Later, she had taught herself to catch small game. She was not a particularly skillful hunter, but skillful enough. Besides, she needed little. And once she found her way back to her tribe, she would be safe.

She reviewed her needs. The first, without a doubt, was shelter. If a blizzard caught her in the open, she would die.

Shiva looked around her. It was cold here in the upper reaches of the cave, but deeper in it would be warmer. Not warm, never warm, but warmer. And however chill the breath of Mamar on the surface, in the deep cave it would never grow any colder. She knew this from experience of the forest warrens of her secret friends.

Of course, she was forbidden to enter the caves. The tribal taboo was long-standing and clear. The caves were prohibited to any single member of the tribe; to any two members of the tribe. Only groups of three or more might enter safely. Like most taboos, this one had two aspects. It protected against stumbling on a lion or a bear. And it avoided offending the ancestors. The ancestors lived in the deep caves, and only a Crone might speak with them.

She would be Crone. The thought hung in her mind, a wonder and a precious thing. She would be Crone. She turned the idea over gently like a rare and fragile egg, as if on thinking of the possibility before, she had not really believed it, but she believed it now.

She found herself wondering what it would be like to be a Crone. Magic frightened her, as magic frightened most members of her tribe, but perhaps she would not be frightened when she became a Crone. Perhaps knowing the magic took away the fear, as knowing the spirits took away the fear of conversing with them. As Crone she would talk with spirits, converse with the spirits of the ancestors. She might even talk with her mother and her father.

The excitement flared so violently in Shiva, she could scarcely catch her breath. Shiva had never known her father, who was taken by a lion a moon or more before she was born. She had never known her mother, who had died giving her life. Over the years she had made pictures in her mind, imagining a woman and a man who were her mother and her father. She had spoken with these imaginings and sometimes found that they spoke back to her. But it was not the same, had never been the same. These creations of her mind were whispers in her ear, shimmerings beyond the eye, vague pictures that sometimes went their own way and sometimes not. At times she had wondered if these pictures in her mind might be actual spirits; and at times she had pretended that they were. But deep in her heart she knew they could not be. What would it be like to meet the spirit of her mother in living reality?

She felt the pounding of her heart and pushed her thoughts in a different direction to still it. She could not afford to let her mind wander now. If she was to survive, she must think—and think clearly—only of the matter at hand.

Beyond the forest of ice pillars, beyond the frozen waterfall, beyond the niche where she had thought the Crone crouched, there was a dark opening that might take her downward into the more sheltered depths. It was from here she heard the sound of dripping water, a clear indication that the cave ran deeper, for at this level all water was completely frozen into ice.

But before she dared explore, she needed light, for the light in the upper reaches of the cavern would not extend below. For light she needed fire. And for fire she needed wood.

Moving cautiously—for to slip might cause an injury, and here an injury was certain death—she began to climb upward to the light and the entrance of the cave.

The climb was not difficult, despite the skin of ice on much of the rocky surface. She clambered across an apron of loose rubble, saw the entrance loom large before her, then popped from the cave like a badger from its set.

Mamar's Kingdom. The world stretched desolate on every side, a desert of rock and frost and ice; and beyond, in a hollow, a snowfield devoid of a single animal track. The cavern entrance was on high ground, so she could see a great distance over this flat sweep of land. Her heart jumped, for she saw at once that there was wood.

The growth was stunted, but there was definitely growth. She saw low, spreading willow, patches of birch shrub and even juniper. But most exciting of all was the clump of cassiope. She knew that plant, with its white, bell-shaped flowers in summer and its distinctively shaped tiny leaves. It was an evergreen, so full of pungent resin that it would burn when wet.

Once she set it alight, she would have illumination to explore the inner cavern. But more to the point, there was enough willow to build her a fire. Birch bark was oily and would make good kindling. A birch branch split and feathered would burn strongly, like the cassiope, even when wet. Once started, she could use her fire to dry out more wood. There was little here, but there was enough to build at least one fire, and if she searched farther afield, she might find more. Mamar had proved kind. She would be warm.

Her whole instinct was to run from the cave mouth and begin the trek home, but she controlled it. If she had learned nothing else in her short, eventful life, she had learned caution. Those who acted without thought often died.

Vigilance and foresight were the Mother's fundamental laws. She was very cold and very hungry. If she set out to find her way home now, Mamar would sap her strength and chill her heart before she could cover more than a few miles. She would weaken and grow sleepy. She would lie down in the snow and die.

She was turning as the thoughts went through her mind. Now, suddenly, all movement, all thought stopped. She saw behind her. And gasped.

There was another snowfield, a sweeping plain of white, still and unbroken as the face of death. Beyond it, sparkling, dazzling, towered a cliff of ice so high that its upper reaches were lost in billows of eternal mist. It was a miracle, an impossibility, something huge almost beyond her comprehension. And now that she saw it, she heard it too, a low rumbling, creaking, grinding sound that laid an unrelenting background to the entire scene. It was a wonder. But the most wondrous thing of all was that she had seen this amazing sight before.

The memory flooded through her. There was the sound and the smell of the rhino that had chased her, then the sudden, bone-jarring fall into the long-abandoned den and then the bleached

87

white skull of Saber resting on its ledge.

It was a jumble that created a tangle of emotions. Saber was a cat of myth, a monster of the dreamtime grown so large that he was banished by the Mother. Saber was ancient magic, a cat so enormous he dwarfed a male cave lion, with teeth to rival a mammoth's tusks. No living eye had ever seen Saber, no living ear ever heard his mighty roar. No hunter ever claimed to have sighted Saber's spoor.

Yet Shiva had discovered Saber's skull. There had been no doubt. Even the rich and powerful Barradik tribe, who wished beyond all things to claim that the skull was not the skull of Saber, had been able to convince no one but themselves.

In the dry, disused and gloomy den, with the rhino still snorting and snuffling short-sightedly outside, Shiva had stared into the eyeless sockets of that giant skull and experienced a waking dream.

In this dream she had seen the living Saber. He was a tusked tiger so enormous that he stood higher than her head. He had walked the tundra proudly, fearful of nothing, and behind him had reared the same ice cliff that blocked her whole horizon now.

She shivered. What did it mean? Did Saber's

descendants still stalk Mamar's Kingdom?

Shiva pushed that idea from her mind as well. If Saber stalked here, there was nothing she could do about it except try to avoid the great, dangerous beast. For now, she had enough to do in order to survive.

Again she reviewed her position. She had a cave for immediate shelter, almost certainly a deep cave for additional protection. She had wood and kindling to make a fire that would give her light and warm her bones. Food must be next.

She suspected there would be rabbit. If anything could live here, it was rabbit. And she could, she knew, trap rabbit almost with ease. All the same, she could not survive on rabbit alone. The animal was tasty to eat but bore a curious curse. If you ate rabbit and only rabbit, you sickened and died. Not quickly, but as surely as if you were embraced by a bear. She might eat rabbit, if there were rabbits here, but she must eat something else as well.

She moved away from the cave, her eyes never still, searching. Eventually, a distance away, she found it on the leeward side of a rock. Reindeer moss, a small growth. It was not the most palatable of food, but it was food. And the lichen growing nearby was food too. These would keep her healthy; and if she trapped a rabbit, for a while at least she would not starve.

She gathered some of the moss at once and chewed on it, ignoring the slight bitterness on her tongue. But she did not tarry long. Food was always important, but before food came warmth. Hunger might gnaw at her and weaken her, but hunger worked slowly. If she did not somehow warm the deep chill in her body, she might die in hours, especially if it snowed.

She collected wood first, what little there was, and stored it just inside her cave. Then she stripped some birch bark for kindling and finally gathered a little of the resinous cassiope. She was finished none too soon. As she started back toward the cave, it began to snow.

As the first snow fell, a wind sprang up, and soon the landscape was blotted out by a whirling storm. But by then Shiva was squatted well inside the cave mouth, her little haul of wood and kindling well protected by an overhang of rock. She settled down patiently to make fire.

Fire making was one of the few magic arts that was not exclusive to the Crones. Each tribe had its official firemaster—among the Shingu it was a large man named Shem, with strong hands and an overhanging lip. But it was a ceremonial position. Most of the tribe, excepting the very young and the very stupid, knew how to make fire, although their skill in the art varied. Shiva had the knack, but not easily. Thus hours crawled by as she spun the stick relentlessly between her hands, her concentration never wavering for an instant as she quietly chanted the sonorous fire spell that would call forth flame.

Eventually she saw the barest curl of smoke. She chanted faster, louder, spinning the pointed twig with renewed vigor. Her face was close to the shredded birch bark intermixed with cassiope, and her breath fanned the first spark when it appeared. She watched the pinpoint glow spread slowly, then dart like a tiny orange river through the kindling. The ancient magic worked anew. Flame sprang up to lick the willow branches. For a time it smoldered, flickered, died and then resurrected. But soon it grew strong and sought to eat the wood. Shiva smiled and offered up the ritual prayer of thanks to the Mother Goddess of All Things, who long ago, in the dreamtime, had taught the serpent to make fire. The serpent had taught womankind.

For a while she did no more than huddle over her fire, welcoming the warmth it gave and listening to the storm. She would survive. She was certain now she would survive. She had shelter, she had warmth, she had reindeer moss for food and her skills and her wits to catch more. Even the storm that now piled drifts of snow across the entrance to her cave did not disturb her too much, for she did not believe it would last long. Later there would be great storms, lasting days and nights. But not yet, not even in Mamar's Kingdom. Soon the Ice God would quiet again, perhaps even sleep for a time. And after the storm the sky might clear, bringing sun.

Wind eddies carried errant flakes of snow into the cave to hiss in her now-blazing fire, reminding her that her present position was purely temporary. She needed to push more deeply into the cave for safety. She was being wasteful of her wood, and though she did not regret it, for her need of warmth was great, she knew it was only prudent to save as much wood as she could carry for her journey.

How far was she from the village of her tribe? Some instinct told her she might not be far—a day's march, perhaps. They must have brought her here, as far as she could tell, in little more than a single night. But even if the distance was short, her problem remained. How would she find the way? A single mistake and she would trek away from her destination, not toward it. A single mistake and she would plunge deeper into Mamar's Kingdom, where Death waited patiently to greet her.

Her thoughts became indistinct as she stared into the flickering fire, luxuriating in the warmth that crept through every fiber of her body. The flames seemed slowly to grow larger, expanding to fill her entire mental horizon. She felt her eyelids droop.

Explore the cave, her mother's voice commanded.

Shiva's eyes snapped open, and she started so violently that a muscle cramped in her left calf. She stretched her leg to ease it and looked around her fearfully. But she knew there was no one there.

Explore the cave. The message had been as clearly spoken as if her mother squatted by her shoulder.

Shiva pushed herself to her feet, reluctant to leave the heat but well aware what she must do. Taking a blazing branch to act as a torch, she made her way back and down to the forest of pillars and the frozen waterfall where she had first awakened in Mamar's Ice Kingdom. Then she moved to the dark tunnel beyond. It was a passage downward.

Cautious as always, Shiva picked her way carefully. In the flickering light of her torch, she discovered the passageway was formed in a natural series of broad, shallow steps. It carried her gently downward, farther and farther, until she wondered if it might ever end. Then suddenly the passage opened into another cavern.

Shiva stepped out and held the torch high. The cave was well below the depth for ice to form, adequately ventilated yet completely guarded against the chill winds of Mamar's savage breath. Nor was it overlarge. If she chose to carry fire and wood here, it would grow pleasantly warm. There was even a high fissure that might act as a natural chimney to take away the smoke.

She walked over to examine it and stopped. There were ashes of a dead fire, some charred wood immediately beneath the fissure. Someone had been here before her, someone who had lit a fire.

For a long time Shiva remained where she was, staring down at those dead ashes. She was not the first. Of course she was not the first. But had she who had come before her been tested as a Crone? It did not matter. The very presence of that old fire peeled away her isolation. She felt less alone and was grateful. Was this why the spirit of her mother had urged her to explore the cave? It seemed entirely likely, for isolation bred fear, and fear could kill as easily as Mamar's breath.

She was about to return to the upper level when she noticed a second passageway leading from the little cave, narrower than the one by which she had entered. Best to explore this too, she thought, while her torch still burned strongly. There was no scent of any animal, nor did she really expect to meet with anything particularly dangerous, but it did no harm to be sure. She walked across the cave and squeezed into the second passage.

It widened almost at once and climbed sharply; then, just as her legs began to ache, she entered a cavern similar in size to the one she had just left. She halted, her heart leaping in sudden excitement, scarcely able to believe what she was seeing. One thought and one thought only leaped full-blown into her mind: She would live. For a moment she could only stand and stare in the flickering torchlight. There was plenty of firewood and kindling here, enough for her journey and more. And with it a firestone, so that she might call up the magic spark quickly.

And there was food. She saw the reindeer moss at once—much more than she had collected—and with it nuts and berries, dried out but good to eat. A moment later her eyes fell upon a deep niche in one wall and she saw the meat: frozen carcasses of rabbit, hare, fox and a plump, peculiar short-winged bird she did not recognize. Some were partly eaten, most untouched, and all were fresh as the day that they had been put in this chill store.

Even if her journey lasted many days, she had the means for her survival. This food and firewood must have been left for her by the Crone: a test of her luck or diligence in finding it. She felt almost light-headed with relief. And hard on the heels of her relief came the bottomless sensation that crawled so close to panic. What if her mother's spirit had not spoken to her? What if she had not explored?

But she had explored; and she would explore further to ensure there was nothing here she might miss. Perhaps the Crone had hidden weapons too. With food and fire, a flint knife and perhaps an axe, she would have everything she needed.

She found the crawl space almost at once. It

climbed upward steeply, not narrow but with such a low roof that she had to bend double and in places crawl on hands and knees to negotiate it. After a few moments her whole body ached and she could distinctly feel the cold increasing once again. Soon there was ice underfoot and clinging in glistening patches to the walls. She found herself wondering if she should go on, but somehow she knew she must. Almost at once the crawl space became a passage, so that at last she could stand comfortably upright. The passage twisted around a bend and ended.

Shiva stifled the scream but could not control the gasp that sudden terror ripped from her throat. She was in another cave, a bubble in the rock no more than a few paces across, higher up and far more chill than any she had seen so far. A row of silent, staring women was little more than an arm's length away from her.

There were seven of them. Each wore a strip of bearskin wrapped around her upper arm. Each was dead, propped upright against the wall, her body perfectly preserved by the cold of Mamar's Kingdom. Caught in the flicker of the torchlight, the sightless eyes gazed into Shiva's own.

8

Desperation

It was snowing hard now, so there was worried talk about the fate of the hunt. Hiram ignored it. His practiced eye told him the storm would be short-lived. Later, perhaps even soon, there would be blizzards lasting days, but not quite yet. In a few hours at most this one would be over. The hunters would leave their temporary shelters and return to camp.

But if the storm posed little danger to the hunt, it was a disaster beyond measure to Hiram. He was himself a skillful hunter, capable of tracking the most wary game, capable, perhaps, of tracking Shiva where the women had taken her. But not now. Not when all signs had been obliterated by the snow.

She was in Mamar's Kingdom. Why she had

been taken there he did not know, for the Crone, when she had awakened from her trance, had been angry and would tell him nothing. But Mamar's Kingdom lay to the north, and if he moved quickly, before the great snows came, he would have little trouble reaching it. But having reached it, what then? She might be anywhere in the wasteland.

He waited, squatting by the fire built near the entrance in the house of men. He stared out at the flakes of snow swirling and curling in the cold air. The wounds from the cut on his arm had begun to heal on their own, and he ignored their dull throbbing. Little of his inner turmoil showed on his face.

There was nothing he could do until the snow stopped. As a hunter he knew patience. Thus he squatted and waited and tried not to think how many ways a girl like Shiva might die in Mamar's Kingdom.

Why had the women taken her? A test, his mother had said. As had the Crone. But what sort of test? It was beyond his comprehension, as most things women did were.

He had heard Shiva's voice issue from the mouth of the Crone, like the voice of a spirit. Did this mean Shiva was already dead? Yet what she said, what the Crone said, made little sense if she was not still alive. And if alive, she could not live for long; not alone in Mamar's Kingdom.

The snow was easing. Hiram felt no surprise, no elation, simply the certainty that the storm would be over soon. He even knew the sky would clear, at least for a time. It had been a light enough fall for the season, one that would not make the going too difficult. With luck and good judgment he could still reach Mamar's Kingdom before the great snows came. But what was the point of reaching Mamar's Kingdom if he could not track her?

He thought of one who could track her. Hiram pushed the thought aside. He stood and walked past the fire, out of the house of men. The wind had died, and all that was left of the storm were a few large, errant flakes. He looked around him at a village camp turned white.

A great fear held Hiram motionless. Around him the camp was coming alive again after the brief storm. Women were moving about their business. He could no longer ignore the thought: There was one who could track her.

It was worse than his fear of magic or his fear of women. It was the greatest of all his fears, yet one he must face now, for his love of Shiva.

The memory that engulfed him was a smell, the rank stench of an ogre warren. He had been dragged there by one of the monsters, taken into a cavern where the monsters assembled. He had seen these nightmare creatures closer than almost any human had for generations. He had seen the muscular bodies, the thick matted hair, the frowning brow ridge in the distorted skull, the massive teeth and jaws. He had heard their growls and grunts as they had discussed his fate. He had felt the gaze of their dark eyes on him, filled with hate.

Yet these brutes were Shiva's friends. He had not understood it then, he could not understand it now, but he knew it to be true. Shiva walked with impunity in the deep forest. Shiva entered the ogre warrens and was unafraid.

She knew their names. The ogre chief was Thag—the same creature who had kidnapped Hiram. His son, a special friend to Shiva, was called Doban. His mate was Hana, his advisor Hagar, his great rival Shil. Shiva knew them and talked of them as if they were human beings. Shiva loved them. But that was not the wonder. The wonder was that they loved Shiva too.

It had taken Hiram a long time to accept it. Ogres were ogres, monsters who had warred with humankind in ancient days. He knew they were baby stealers, brain eaters, creatures of such evil that even the Mother would not acknowledge them as her own. For all that, there were ogres who loved Shiva. They welcomed her to their caverns, sheltered her, protected her and fed her. Once, when she had been taken by the Barradik, they had come by the hundreds to save her.

Hiram's feet moved of their own accord and began to carry him away from the village camp. If the great snows came now, sooner than he expected, he would die. But that made no difference. He loved Shiva. He had to find her, and there was one who could track her.

Shiva talked with Hiram more than with any other in the tribe. Often she talked of the ogres, trying to persuade him they were not the monsters he thought. She would tell him how little Hana ruled the mighty Thag as easily as a mammoth might rule a hare. She talked fondly of Doban, almost fully grown now, who, as a boy, had saved her from a wolf. And she spoke of others in the clan whom she had gotten to know and like, ogres with their own peculiarities and quirks, strengths and weaknesses, and special talents.

The snowfall was not so deep that it prevented

102

his breaking into the hunter's trot, a steady, jogging run he could keep up for hours. Most game could outrun a hunter easily over a short distance, but with patience and the hunter's trot, Hiram could eventually exhaust a deer. It was second nature to him now, used whenever there were great distances to be covered.

He emerged from the foothills onto the plain, his body comfortably warm beneath his furs, his feet leaving an obvious trail behind him in the snow. He moved with confidence and seemingly little effort, not quickly but relentlessly. He tried not to think where he was going.

There were ogres who had special talents. Shiva had often talked in something close to awe of Heft the Hunter.

Hiram had never seen Heft, as far as he knew. But he knew this ogre was a legend in the ogre clan. Heft was a special friend of Thag, the ogre chief, but that was not and never had been his claim to fame. Heft, quite simply, could track any game, for any distance, across any terrain. He could follow trails that others could not see. He could pick up scent in water—an impossibility, of course, but Shiva said it was definitely so. When Doban, as a child, was lost, Heft found him though the trail had long gone cold.

If any creature on the Mother's earth could find Shiva in the barren wasteland of Mamar's Kingdom, that creature must be Heft the Hunter.

Time blurred as Hiram's mind locked into the rhythm of the hunter's trot. Mile followed mile beneath his feet, his senses barely aware of the countryside around him. The familiar feel of steady movement dulled his fears.

He had no doubt that he could find Heft the Hunter. He had, after all, been in the forest and been taken to the ogre warrens. Only once, thank goodness, but once was enough. He might not be able to track like Heft, but Hiram was himself a hunter, knowledgeable in the hunter's ways. Once taken, he could find his way again. Besides which Shiva, for amusement, had taught him the elements of ogre signs. He knew the markings made by the monsters to blaze their forest trails. He would find them: perhaps not quite as quickly as he might have liked, but he would find them.

But he was not sure how he would approach the ogres. They did not know him as they knew Shiva. They might look on him and simply think of him as food.

He did not know Heft by sight, but there was one he did know. Hiram shivered. He would never forget the nightmare face of Thag, the monster who had carried him—carried him as easily as a man might carry a rabbit—through the forest. Thag, as he now knew, was chieftain of his clan and respected for his strength and ferocity. And Thag was the special friend of Heft the Hunter. He just needed to reach Thag.

Hiram rested, squatting with his back against a rock. Sweat, built up during the long run, chilled pleasantly on his body beneath the furs. His breath plumed and froze in sparkling crystals on the hood fur near his mouth. Overhead the sky had cleared exactly as he had predicted. A weak sun shone down on him, reflecting brightly from the white snowscape all around.

He knew some words of ogre speech. No one had believed ogres to be capable of speech, but Shiva had changed that—as Shiva, now that he came to think of it, had changed so much. She spoke the ogre tongue with fluency and had even managed to teach a few of her more cunning ogre friends to converse with human speech. And she had taught him, too. Only a few words, a very few (and not well pronounced, from what she told him), but they might be enough. If he found the ogres, he could demand to be brought to Thag. Surely they would not kill him right away when they discovered he knew their tongue and knew their chief.

Hiram pushed himself back to his feet and set off again, falling at once into the hunter's trot. He did not really want to think about his next problem. If all ogres frightened him, Thag frightened him most of all. In fact Thag terrified him. He was an ogre among ogres: big, brutal, bad-tempered, unpredictable and horrifyingly strong. Thag liked Shiva, that much Hiram knew. But would he listen long enough to learn that Shiva was in danger, to do what needed to be done?

Inside his own head, Hiram shrugged. He would have to make Thag understand, for if he did not, Shiva would die. Her only hope now was Heft the Hunter.

Hiram trotted onward, his mind numb with worry and with fear. Soon he was in sight of the forest where the ogres made their lair.

9

Face of Death

Shiva backed away in horror. She had seen death before—many times—but never like this. There was no mark on any of the women, no injury, no sign of sickness nor of wound. Their faces seemed almost serene. Their eyes were open, the moisture in them filmed whitely into ice. Over them hung a stillness so profound, it seemed impossible to break.

She wanted to turn, to scramble back along the crawl space, to flee these horrid corpses, but she did not. Instead she waited while her heartbeat dropped slowly back to normal and forced herself to think.

None of the women was Shingu. One had the broad, flat features of the eastern Menerrum.

Another was tall enough to be a Thorangando. A third had the look and coloring of a Barradik. Different women, different tribes, but none a Shingu.

They had been placed with care in their icy tomb, set formally one beside the other, shoulder to shoulder, facing the entrance. Yet between the fourth and the fifth there was a gap. Such careful placing of the rest; and yet a gap.

How had these women died? Not mauled by any beast, for their bodies were entirely intact. Not starved, for there was ample food below; and besides, only the Thorangando was thin, and this was characteristic of her tribe. Had Mamar chilled their life force with his bitter breath? But all were well wrapped in skins and furs, all looked strong enough to resist the cold.

Who were they? A Menerrum, a Thorangando, a Barradik, four others, perhaps from different tribes. They had one thing in common: Each wore a strip of bearskin on her arm. The Crone had said: *You will be the next Crone of the Shingu tribe. That is why I have marked you with the bearskin band.* These were not Shingu, but they wore the band. Were they too marked as future Crones, Crones of their own tribes? It seemed it must be so. But if it was so, then each had failed her test.

108

Seven women, perhaps from seven tribes, each put to the test as Crone, each dead now without a mark. But how had they died? It was the only question of importance.

Honesty compelled her to admit she did not know. But the answer must be there if she had the courage to look for it. Before her terror could build further, she forced herself forward, reached out and touched the nearest corpse.

It was the body of the tall Thorangando. Her fingers touched the face and found it chill and hard, like rock or ice. Perhaps these women had been chilled by Mamar's breath.

Shiva took a deep breath, whispered an apology to the woman's spirit, and began to unwrap the skins and furs from the body. If there was a hidden wound, she must know. But with the furs removed and an examination made, there was no wound, no bruise, no injury: nothing to suggest a cause of death. Shiva licked her lips nervously and replaced the woman's clothes. She glanced across at the other bodies, wondering if she should repeat the investigation. She decided against it. All must have died the same way. If there were no marks on one, there would be no marks on any. As she suspected, Mamar, God of Ice, had killed them.

There was food. There was shelter. There was wood. There was the means of making fire. None of it had been enough. Mamar murdered those who trespassed into his Kingdom. As he would kill Shiva too if she failed to outwit him.

Cautiously, taking care not to touch any other of the bodies, Shiva searched. There was nothing else in the chamber and no other exit. With her torch burning low, she returned to the crawl space. Although the worst of the intense fear had left her, she was profoundly disturbed. There were so many questions that cried out for an answer: Had the seven women come here separately or together? Had they died singly? Had they failed in their attempt to become Crone and crawled into that hidden cave to die?

She was not, she realized suddenly, thinking clearly. It was ridiculous to imagine the women had died in that little chamber. There was no natural posture of death. They were set in a line, shoulder to shoulder, backs against the wall. The position of the bodies had been arranged.

She reached the storeroom, collected some wood and kindling, then moved on to set a fire in the dead ashes by the natural chimney in the other cave. She lit it with the dying embers of her torch and waited while it flared. There was

110

an updraft that persuaded it to flare almost at once, and the wood, well dried, burned fiercely with strong heat. Her instinct had been correct. Within minutes, the cave was warm.

Shiva went back to the store cavern. She had found no weapons, but she managed to split a piece of stone with a sharp enough edge to hack some meat from the carcass of a hare. She brought it back, speared the meat roughly with a convenient branch, then squatted to hold it in the leaping flames. In a moment the rich smell of roasting filled the air.

She was, she found, far too hungry to let it cook completely. As she withdrew her makeshift spit, the meat fell off and she had to rescue it from the ashes. She dusted it off and began to eat voraciously, finding it seared on the outside and bloody in the middle. No matter. She had eaten raw meat before now.

The food warmed and comforted her but did not, once the edge was taken from her hunger, divert her mind from the mystery of the women in their frozen cavern grave. Something about the way they had been arranged preyed on her mind, tormenting her. Yet she could not quite think what it was.

She was brooding on the mystery overlong.

111

The temptation to remain in this deep cave was strong. But Shiva knew, as surely as if she had been told by the Hag, that if she stayed within the caves, she was lost. The obvious and easy option was death: death postponed, but death inevitably. The food and the firewood were a subtle trap. She might eat well and huddle by the fire, but however well she husbanded supplies, they would not carry her through the entire winter. And when they ran out, there would be no chance at all of foraging for more in the season of blizzards. To stay would not merely mean she failed her test. To stay was to die.

Was this what had happened to the other women? Had they remained thoughtlessly in these caverns until the winter had trapped them? Somehow she did not think so. Certainly they had not starved: The condition of the bodies was mute testament to that. And even without fire, the cold would not have killed them so quickly if they had remained in the shelter of the deeper cave.

No, Shiva thought, they had seen the trap, as she had seen it. They had, perhaps, remained a little while as she had, eating from the stored food and burning the stored wood. But then they would have left the caves as she must leave the caves. The only real safety lay in accepting danger. She must brave Mamar's Kingdom and find her way back to her tribe quickly.

And this, she was certain, was what the other women had tried to do. Except that they had failed. Somewhere out there in the Ice God's Kingdom they had died. Perhaps caught in a blizzard, perhaps smothered in a drift, perhaps simply unable to withstand the all-pervading chill. And someone had brought their bodies back here, one after another, with reverence, and left them in the cavern tomb.

She did not want to leave the caves, but knew she must. The only question was when. The great snows had not yet come but would come soon. And before them there would be the little snows, the storms that blew themselves out in an hour or so but still required her to take shelter while they raged.

She doubted she was more than a day distant from her tribe. She had been carried here while drugged, so it was unlikely to be any further. But that did not mean she could reach her tribe in a day, for she still had to find them. If she did not find them before the great snows came, she would die.

There was only one sensible conclusion. She

must leave at once. She was warm. She had fed. She could carry with her food and firewood from the store. There was no better time.

She left the fire to return to the store and cut herself a supply of meat, which she left beside the reindeer moss. Then, fighting back her distaste, she reentered the crawl space carrying a fresh brand from the fire.

The women watched her enter with dead eyes. Four were shoulder to shoulder, then came a space, then three. She knew now what the space was for. If she failed, there was no forgiveness. Her body would be set in that space along with the others to wait and watch for the next who would be tested as a Crone.

Shiva wedged her torch into a crevice and began, with great deliberation, to move from one body to another. She felt nervousness, but little fear. The spirits of these women were long gone to the dreamtime. They had no further use for the bodies they had left behind, let alone their old possessions. But Shiva had use for them. She selected the warmest furs and exchanged them for her own clothing. Then she took some skins to make a pouch. And finally, toward the end of a careful search, she found what she had hoped she might: a finely chipped flint blade strapped to the leg of one of the women. She had a knife now, a weapon.

"Thank you," Shiva whispered formally, wondering, not for the first time, if her voice might carry to the dreamtime. Then she left the chill rock tomb, painfully aware that if she ever returned, it would be as a corpse.

Below, in the store cave, she carved more of the half-frozen meat using her new blade, wrapping it with the rest and a compact supply of the moss in the skin pouch she had made. In the neighboring cavern she warmed herself one final time at the remnants of her dying fire, added firewood to the store she was to carry, then climbed out of the cave.

The sky had cleared after the earlier storm and sunshine turned the snow-covered world into a dazzle that was almost blinding. Shiva pulled a lighter skin over her head to act as a hood, drawing it across so that the shaggy fur hung down to shield her eyes. Her world was a featureless snowfield now, bewildering and alien, and while the snow might melt a little if the sky remained clear, she knew she could not wait. Every hour was precious to her now.

Which way should she go? Mamar's Kingdom lay to the north. Thus her tribe had made camp somewhere to the south. She would find them easily enough once she could see the mountains, but for the moment her horizon was flat and featureless except for the gigantic ice cliff beyond her cave. She must trek south, but where was south?

Shiva selected a straight branch about a full stride long from her original store of firewood and stuck it upright in the snow. She noted where its shadow ended and marked the spot with another, smaller stick. Then she retreated into the mouth of the cave again and waited, dulling her impatience.

The shadow crept away from the first mark she made, so slowly she could not follow its progress unless she looked away. Time crawled. Shiva squatted motionless, her eyes downcast beneath the fur fringing of her hood. Eventually she rose again, walked out and marked where the shadow ended now. It was done. She stood at the first marker stick and faced toward the second, knowing from the tribal lore that she now looked east. She turned to her right hand and set off south without a moment's hesitation.

10

Thag in Peril

Thag hurt. His head ached. His shoulders ached. His legs ached. His useless arm felt as though it were on fire, sending waves of agony through his entire body as he moved. Worse, he felt weak. For the first time in as long as he could remember, he was no longer strong. His muscles trembled like those of an infant or an old, old man. He was forced to rest often, his tired back propped against the trunk of some great tree. He wanted to lie down, to sleep in order to escape the pain. But he knew he did not dare. Shil's men were hunting him.

He had given it to Og-nar. And with one blow: weak though he was, with one blow! He was pleased about that, for he disliked Og-nar almost as much as he disliked Shil. But the others had come after him. They were not supposed to. He was only banished. But they were coming, and he knew why they were coming.

They were clumsy hunters. The first change of wind had brought him the scent of Led and Metrak. Only minutes later his nose told him that Dag the Flint Chipper was with them. They were searching awkwardly for his signs.

At another time he would have ignored them. He would have hidden his signs and traveled slowly. Or allowed them to find his signs and traveled so quickly that they would have fallen from exhaustion trying to keep up.

Not now. Now there was snow, which made signs difficult to hide. Now he was weak and shaken and could not think clearly to hide his sign. Now he could not move quickly. He was the one coming close to exhaustion.

There was a pain when he breathed. Often his head would swing and twist around and around although he was not moving it at all. He felt sick and wanted to throw up, as someone does when he has eaten bad meat. But he could not throw up because of the pain.

He wished they had given him a knife. With a knife he could cut off his useless arm which

118

burned now and threatened to set his whole body on fire.

He leaned against another tree, his head thrown back. There were sounds above him in the upper terraces of the forest. Small, tree-climbing animals bounded about their little lives. Or perhaps the birds watched him. There were not many birds in winter, but there were always some, especially the carrion eaters that watched for things to die. They stayed in the forest in winter because so many things did die then. What a feast he would make for a carrion bird.

Thag pulled himself together with an enormous effort. Years of habit still called his attention to the approaching sounds. They were getting nearer—much nearer—Led and Metrak and Dag. He could not see them yet, but he knew they would carry clubs and probably flint blades.

He moved away from the tree and stumbled through a clump of dense undergrowth, appalled by the noise he made and could not stop himself from making. He sounded like a bear crashing through the shrub.

He stopped, sure they must hear him. But the muffled sounds of their approach did not change. They were still searching ponderously for his signs, still unable to hear him yet however much

119

he crashed and smashed and broke branches like a bear.

Shil should not have done this. Some of the old rage rose up in Thag and helped to dampen the pain. It was not right. It was not proper. It was not *tradition*. Shil should not be chief, for he had cheated in the fight. And even if he was chief, he should not have sent Thag into exile. And even if he had sent Thag into exile, he should not have sent his men after him.

It was strange, Thag thought, how much Shil had dared. The entire clan might have turned against him for cheating, for ignoring the tradition and ordering the exile. But the clan had not, even though Thag's exile at this time of year and with one arm useless was almost certain death.

Almost certain death was not good enough for Shil. He had sent his men to hunt Thag down and murder him. At least he had not dared do that within sight of the clan.

Thag stared down at his great feet, whimpering a little in the back of his throat at the pains in his shoulder, his chest and head that made thinking so difficult. "You are *stupid*!" he told his feet severely. "You run and run, and soon you will be too tired to run anymore and they will catch you, and when they catch you, they will kill you."

120

Because, he thought, you are too tired. They could not kill you if you were fresh and free from pain. Not idiots like Led and Metrak and Dag the Flint Chipper.

His head began to spin again, and he ignored the pain in his chest to take deep breaths to stop the way the forest turned around him. And as the spinning slowed, a thought crawled into his head like a black beetle from the forest floor: If he continued to run from them, he would die. He would exhaust himself and they would catch him and club him.

He was, he discovered, on his knees, hugging himself with his one good arm. He, Thag, the strongest of the clan, was on his knees.

Thag's head went back, his lips curled from the broad, strong teeth. A muted roar erupted from his throat. They would not drive him to his knees! Not Led, not Metrak, not Dag the Flint Chipper, not all three together, not even if they were they joined by Shil, the false chief who cheated in a fight. He pushed himself savagely to his feet. "Here!" he roared so loudly that the carrion birds in the upper terraces took flight in panic. "I am here! I, Thag, am *here* and Shil eats *dung*!"

They heard him. Even imbeciles like those

121

three could not miss that call. He listened to them blundering in his direction, drawn by his shout. Suddenly he felt very calm, and though the pain was high in him, somehow it did not matter.

With great deliberation, preserving his energy, protecting his broken body from the pain, Thag climbed onto a branch that overhung the trail. And waited.

They came exactly as he had thought they would: Led and Metrak together in the lead and Dag the Flint Chipper, sniffing like a dog, glancing all about him like a bird, many paces behind.

If the wind changed, they would scent him. If the wind changed, he was dead. If they looked up, they would see him. If they looked up, he was dead.

The wind did not change. They did not glance upward. Led and Metrak passed below him at a steady trot, so close he might have reached down to touch their hair. Each carried a club and a spear.

Thag waited as they disappeared around a bend in the trail ahead, then gently turned his head to watch Dag weave and bob toward him. Like the others, he was armed, a club in one hand, an axe-head in the other. He passed below the branch.

122

Despite his pain, Thag grinned—and dropped on him.

Dag went down without a sound, his eyes wide with surprise. Thag circled his head with his one good arm and jerked. There was a sound like the snapping of a twig and Dag went limp. Thag dragged himself from the body, picked up Dag's fallen club and melted into the forest.

It took them a long time to realize the Flint Chipper was no longer with them. And, when they did, longer still to decide what to do next. Thag watched them from a clump of bushes as they stood debating the situation in a tiny clearing.

"He may have lost his way," suggested Metrak.

"How could he have lost his way—he was right behind us!" Led snarled.

"Do you think something's happened to him?" Metrak asked.

"What could happen to him?"

"A bear might have hugged him."

"The bears are asleep, idiot!" snapped Led. "The bears are asleep until the summer."

Not this bear, Thag thought, grinning. *This bear stayed awake to hug him!*

"A boar then," Metrak said.

"We would have heard, wouldn't we? You can

hear a boar a long way."

They stood staring vaguely around them. Eventually Metrak said, "Do you think we should go back and look for him?"

Led thought about it for a minute. "Yes," he said. "Thag can wait. He can't move fast anyway. You go back and look for Dag the Flint Chipper. I'll stay here and wait for you."

"All right," Metrak said. He trotted from the clearing.

Thag waited until the sounds of his departure faded, then stepped out from the bushes. He carried Dag's club in his good hand. Led, who was staring after Metrak, did not at once see him. Thag padded forward silently. When he was within arm's reach of Led, he growled softly, far back in his throat. Led spun around, his jaw dropping.

"Hello, Led," Thag said, and struck him behind the ear with Dag's club. Led dropped without a sound.

It was simply done, but the effort, nonetheless, made Thag's head spin. He stood over Led's crumpled form swaying slightly, his eyes moving in and out of focus. After a moment, Led groaned, rolled and began to pull himself painfully back to his feet. Thag knew he should

124

hit him again, but he could not. Led seemed to have retreated to the end of a long tunnel, out of reach.

"Help!" Led screamed. "He's here, Metrak! Thag is *here!*"

Thag found, thankfully, that his head was clearing, although striking a blow with the club had sent a shock through his body that had made his chest pain flare and started up a vicious throbbing in his useless arm. Nevertheless, he stepped forward.

"Help!" Led screamed again. "He's hitting me! He's murdering me!" He raised his own club and swung it inaccurately in Thag's direction.

Murder, Thag thought, sounded like an excellent idea. Although he would have to do it quickly, before Metrak returned. Led was the smarter of the two and usually gave orders, but he was a cowardly man and useless in a fight. Even in his pain-filled, weakened state, Thag thought he could best him. But Metrak was a different matter.

Thag swung. Led leaped aside, then jumped forward and swung again at Thag with his club. Thag made a small movement—he was incapable at that moment of a large one—and the club whistled past his ear. He struck again, hard.

"Oooow!" howled Led, clutching his arm. He danced around, still howling, making no attempt to strike at Thag again. Which was as well, as Thag was swinging in and out of darkness, his club lowered, his head bowed.

Led stopped howling and dancing. He peered suspiciously toward Thag's swaying figure. "You're on your last legs, Thag," he muttered, and took a cautious step forward.

Thag watched him coming through a haze of dizziness and pain. Led seemed to be moving very slowly, but with a relentless purpose. His face contorted into a slow grimace that might have been a broad, triumphal smile. "This is for Shil," Led said, and raised his club.

Thag brought up his own club in one sudden, violent movement and caught Led beneath the chin with such force that his feet actually left the ground. He landed heavily on his back, and it was obvious he would not be getting up for a very long time.

Thag felt like death. The final effort had come close to toppling him into the black pit of night. He clung to consciousness, caught by a vague amusement at the unreality of the scene. Led did not move. His club was flung from his hand and now rested in the forked branch of a tree. Thag could not see properly. The edges of his vision were dark, and the center of his vision flickered through a blood fog.

He wondered if he had killed Led. He had certainly killed Dag, but that had been a lifetime before. He did not much like killing people, but he could make an exception of Dag and Led. And Shil.

His head was clearing, his vision widening, the overpowering waves of pain receding slightly. He moved slowly forward until he was standing over Led, who was, unfortunately, still breathing.

There was a sound behind him, and he half turned before his world exploded into lightning bolts of pain. His club—Dag's club—dropped from his helpless hand. He teetered and fell heavily across Led's prostrate form, landing on the shoulder of his useless arm. The pain was hideous, yet darkness would not come. He lay helpless, beyond all movement.

Metrak's ugly face stared down at him, grinning.

11

The Ogres' Lair

He could smell them. The entire forest smelled of ogre, a rank stench that oozed from the trees, the shrubs, the leaves, the very ground beneath his feet. Hiram wondered if he was insane for venturing into this ancient nightmare, then thought of Shiva and decided he was not.

Caution was the key, he reassured himself. He must not frighten the ogres. He must not approach them by stealth. He must proceed openly, as a friend might, perhaps singing a carefree song to reassure them. He began to rehearse a carefree song, humming to the rhythm of a tribal ballad, but decided he sounded like an idiot and stopped almost at once.

Still, the thought was correct. He must not approach them by stealth, for if he did, they would take him for an enemy and kill him at once and eat his brains. An open, friendly approach was the thing. "I am friend," he would say in his few halting words of ogre language. "Take me to your chief. I am friend of Thag."

He was not a friend of Thag's, of course, nor did he ever want to be. But his knowledge of the ogre tongue was bleak, and he would have to keep things very simple if he was to be understood at all. Any ogre he met must know the name of Thag, who was so brutal they had made him ogre chief. If he claimed to be a friend to Thag, no other ogre would dare touch him. With any luck at all, he would be taken directly to the chief.

Which was where things might well get difficult. Hiram still woke up sweating in the night from dreams of Thag. Thag was not only big and ugly—all ogres were like that—he was also impatient and bad-tempered. Hiram recalled Thag's habit of hitting anybody who came near him, friend or foe—and hitting trees and rocks if there was nothing softer handy. Worse still, every few minutes Thag would run amok, trying to savage everyone in sight. Shiva claimed Thag was nothing like this at all, but Hiram knew. Hiram had been captured by the ogres once, and he had seen.

Whatever Shiva said, Hiram considered Thag to be a dangerous lunatic. A dangerous ogre lunatic, which was the most dangerous lunatic of all. How was it possible to talk reason to such a creature when you did not even really speak its language?

He almost turned to trot back the way he had come. It was not Thag who was the lunatic, but Hiram. He had to be a lunatic to try what he was trying.

Shiva said some of the ogres could use human speech. The boy Doban, for example, had somehow picked it up when he was captured by the tribe. And Shiva had taught Doban's mother, Hana, and an ogre called Dan and another called Leban and the same Heft the Hunter Hiram needed so desperately now. Had she taught Thag? He could not remember. But somehow he doubted it.

But if Hiram had only a few words of ogre language and Thag could not fathom human speech, what hope was there for Shiva? First, Hiram had to persuade the insanely bad-tempered Thag to listen, to display a little patience, to postpone the pleasures of slaughtering this Weakling Stranger at once. Then Hiram had to explain that Shiva was in danger (making sure that Thag did not imagine Hiram was to blame) and somehow convey the nature of her peril. Then he had to show how Heft the Hunter was the only creature on the Mother's earth with any hope of finding her. Then he had to persuade Thag to organize a rescue. All with only a few words of ogre language.

"Take me to your chief," Hiram rehearsed to the rhythm of the hunter's trot. "I am friend of Thag."

He loathed the forest. Apart from ogres, it was full of whispers, movements, rustlings, a grim and gloomy place where he could never get away from the sensation of a hundred watching eyes. And dangerous as well. There were dark spirits in the forest, and wolf packs and rampaging boars. There were many bears, although at this season, thank goodness, they were all asleep. If anything large and hairy and horrible rushed toward him out of the undergrowth, it would not be a bear.

He was unfamiliar with the forest trails, but his hunter's eyes darted everywhere, absorbing subtle signs. It was tough going. The ogres did not seem to follow clear pathways. Their trails would sometimes break abruptly, as if they plunged into the deep undergrowth. At times like that it was very difficult to pick up the signs again, and Hiram found himself circling aimlessly, attempting to find his way back to more certain pathways. It was during one such bout of nervous, aimless circling that the nightmare began.

He broke, quite abruptly, from the tangle of fern and creeper and thornbushes that grabbed at his furs and stepped onto an open trail. Relief caused him to stride forward a pace or two incautiously, eyes darting for signs, when suddenly he saw the ogre. It was resting, leaning against a tree trunk, staring at him wide eyed, an expression of brute fury imprinted on its ugly face.

"I am friend!" Hiram yelled. "Take me to your chief. I am friend of Thag!"

The monster did not move.

"Friend!" Hiram yelled again. He teetered back a pace or two, desperately fighting down an impulse to run away. "Friend!"

Why did it not speak? Why did it not react? Perhaps he was forming the words wrong. The language of the ogre was a guttural tongue, full of growls and clicks. Shiva had often smiled at his attempts to get it right, and while he thought he had managed the few simple phrases he knew, it was possible that his accent was too bad for the creature to understand.

He chilled, as a new thought occurred to him. Perhaps he was distorting the language so much that the ogre thought he was shouting something else. Not "friend" but something else, such as "pigface" or "Stand up and fight, you hairy grub." Perhaps the ogre word for "pigface" sounded very much like the ogre word for "friend."

With a supreme effort Hiram took control of his emotions. He ordered his feet to cease their nervous shuffling backward, ordered his body to stop shaking, swallowed deeply and said, slowly this time, with enormous care and precision, "Take. Me. To. Your. Chief. I am friend of *Thag!*"

But still the monster did not move. Not a twitch of a nostril. Not a flicker of an eyelid. There was not a sign of breath, no movement of the massive chest. A horrid suspicion began to crawl like the black shape of a giant sloth into Hiram's mind. Cautiously, his own breath momentarily suspended, he stepped forward until he was only a foot or two away from the immobile monster. Still it did not move, and now it seemed to him the huge brown eyes were glazed.

In the most courageous moment of his life, Hiram reached out a hesitant hand and touched it. The ogre slid away from him sideways, air escaping from its lifeless body in a drawn-out sigh. It slumped in an ungainly heap on the forest floor, head twisted so horrifyingly that he knew at once its neck was broken.

Hiram panicked. The body, when he touched it, was not yet completely cold. The ogre was only recently dead, and while Hiram desperately wanted to believe it had died in a fall from a tree, or from illness or old age, he knew beyond a doubt that of all the misfortunes that might befall someone, this ogre had met the very worst of them. This ogre had been murdered, and murdered recently. Which meant the ogre's spirit was still somewhere about, shortsightedly searching for its killer. Hiram, who never wanted anything to do with spirits, wanted even less to do with the spirit of a murdered ogre. Suddenly he turned and ran, blundering mindlessly through undergrowth and bracken, his hands ripped by thorns, his face whipped by branches.

He might have run for minutes or for hours. Pain, fear and anguish distorted time, so it seemed only an instant later that he broke free of the forest into the huge clearing with the towering cliff face he remembered so well. This was the very place he had been carried to that ghastly day when Thag had kidnapped him. The cliff was riddled with caverns, caves and passageways, home to a colony of ogres that was far larger than the Shingu tribe.

There were many ogres in the clearing. They scattered in startled alarm at Hiram's sudden appearance, but began to regroup and move slowly, threateningly, toward him.

"I am friend!" Hiram whispered, hands shaking, heart pounding. "Take me to your chief. I am friend of Thag!"

They stopped at Thag's name.

"Thag," Hiram repeated. "I am friend of Thag."

He saw them look at one another uncertainly.

With a stupendous effort, Hiram smiled. "Thag," he said. "Yes—Thag."

It seemed to work. The ogres shuffled toward him, hands outstretched, although it was impossible to judge anything from their expressions, which appeared as savage as before.

12

Rescue

There was no fire in the deep cave, no light, no sound save for the shallow breathing that told her Doban remained with her somewhere in the darkness. She was still bound, the bonds pulled so tightly that one foot had gone numb and her hands and arms pained her like a wound. At the back of her mind was a growing conviction that Shil planned never to release them but wished instead to leave them in the deep cave until the clan forgot their very existence and they starved.

Or froze, she thought sourly. There was a draft that whispered through the cavern, carrying its own dank tales of winter snows and soaking away the last remnants of miserable warmth that remained in her. The deep caves were a great protection at this time of year, but only if you lit a fire or at least were able to move. Bound, without food or flame, it was impossible to keep warm.

There was a sound so stealthy she wondered if it might be her imagination. She stilled her breathing and listened, her whole being concentrated outward. For a long moment there was nothing. Cautiously, she allowed her body to relax. Then, on the distant edges of perception, the sound came again.

At once Hana's mind began to race with possibilities more immediate than slow death by starvation and cold. Had Shil dispatched one of his cronies to kill them now, while they lay helpless? Shil had cheated in the fight for chief, broken with tradition by casting Thag from the clan. Hagar whispered his suspicions that Shil had also dispatched men to attack Thag in the wilderness. Any man who could contemplate such abominations would certainly not hesitate to kill Thag's mate and child. Especially not in the deep caves, where there was none to witness the extent of his corruption.

Hana began to work at her bonds with renewed vigor. She had little fear for herself—life was full of perils, and one type of death was as good as any other—but the thought that Doban might

be in immediate danger was a very different matter. She had watched over Doban since she had
given birth to him, fed him, clothed him, protected him, even ensured his rescue from the
Weakling Strangers. He was almost full grown
now, a skillful hunter almost as strong as his father, but she could not break the habit of a lifetime. He was her son, hers and Thag's, and when
danger threatened, her whole soul rose up to save
him.

She was tightly tied. The twisted strips of skin
came close to cutting into her flesh. All the same,
there was at least the possibility of escape. With
nothing else to do in this chill darkness, she had
been working the ties against an edge of rock. It
was not particularly sharp, but she had perse-
vered so long that some fraying must have taken
place.

"Someone's coming," Doban whispered in the
darkness.

"Lie still and be quiet!" Hana hissed. She continued to work on her bonds. In the way of the
clans, she made a picture in her mind of their
snapping. There was definitely someone coming:
The subtle sounds were clear now, the more so
because whoever came took little enough care to
hide his approach.

She sensed rather than heard the entry of the looming shadow into the cavern where they lay. Then, just as desperation was driving her toward the edge of frenzy, the wind that whistled through the cavern carried his scent to her nostrils. Doban must have caught it too, for he said at once loudly, "We are here, Heft!"

Heft the Hunter merely grunted. He was moving in utter darkness, using his familiarity with the deep caves as a guide. Now, displaying that disquieting sixth sense that always seemed to lead him to his prey, he advanced unerringly to Hana's side.

"Are you whole, Hana?" he asked quietly, using the clan expression to ask whether she was injured.

"Whole enough," Hana told him drily. "But tied. Doban too," she added.

She felt his arms around her, briefly sharing body heat as friends must do. Then the strong fingers began fumbling with her bonds.

"What has happened, Heft?" Hana asked. "Is there news of Thag?"

"No news," Heft muttered. "Shil still rules." He made it sound like a curse placed on the clan.

"Why are you here?"

"To free you."

139

Hana shook her head impatiently. "Why are you here at this time, Heft? Why not earlier, or later?"

She felt him shrug in the darkness. "Shil's men watched me, for they know me to be a friend to Thag. I waited until they no longer watched me."

"You slipped away?"

"They were distracted."

"Distracted? How?"

Heft sniffed the air, an instinctive hunter's trick to make sure nothing was approaching to disturb him. "A Weakling Stranger has come."

A Weakling Stranger? Why should a Weakling Stranger venture through the forest at this season? She pushed the question from her mind. It made no difference. The Stranger had come and caused a diversion, and that was enough.

"Has it snowed?" she asked Heft. She had lain long in the darkness, unable to judge time, worried by the possibility of snow. If there was heavy snow, even Heft might not be able to track Thag.

"It has not snowed," Heft said.

Hana felt a heady bubble of relief and excitement well up from her stomach. If it had not snowed and Heft could release them and they managed to creep from the caverns while Shil's men were distracted by the Weakling

Stranger, there was a possibility they might yet save Thag.

Her numb foot began suddenly to pain her as her bonds loosened; then, just as suddenly, her hands were free. She stretched luxuriantly, welcoming the sharp new pains movement produced. "Doban," she whispered urgently. "Free Doban." But Heft had already left her and was working on the bindings of her son.

"You'll help us find Thag?" Hana asked.

"Yes."

"Do you—" But the question remained unfinished. There was a flurry of movement in the darkness, then Doban was embracing her and Heft embracing them both. If only Thag were here to join them, the moment would be blissful.

It was Hana who broke away. "There is no time," she said. "Hagar told me Shil may have sent men after Thag."

Heft snorted. "We go," he said simply.

She felt him take her hand and reached instinctively for Doban's. Together they moved from the cavern, Heft leading them as surely as if he carried a torch for light.

The deep caverns lay underground and were seldom used, even in winter. Above them ran the tunnels and caves that were the living quarters of the Clan, silent and deserted now, dimly illuminated by the dying embers of the night fires. Above these lay the exits and the upper galleries of the cliff face, a gloomy dappling of light and shade created by the dim, chill, gray-green glow that filtered inward from the entrances. There were far more people at this level, and Heft cautiously kept the little party to the shadows. Hana noted with a certain satisfaction how silently Doban moved. He was developing many useful skills.

They followed a circuitous route to emerge from the cliff face by way of an entrance almost totally concealed by a large bush. Their noses told them no one was near, but all the same Heft halted cautiously to peer out through the branches. Hana moved to his side and saw at once how he had managed their rescue so easily.

At the far side of the clearing a seething, excited mass of clansfolk surrounded the new Rock of Judgment, their attention riveted on the squatting Shil—and on something else she could not see: presumably the Weakling Stranger. She noted with distaste that Shil was surrounded by more club-wielding guards than ever, with new faces among them. It was ever thus. However unpopular a man might be, he always drew additional support on becoming chief. If he survived as chief for any length of time, the majority of the clan might well come to support him. This was the great strength of the chief's position, the reason why, once a man became chief, he grew increasingly difficult to depose. Except by cheating, Hana thought sourly.

It was obvious that Heft had picked his time superbly well. With the attention of the clan so firmly focused on the Weakling Stranger, it would be easy to slip away. Once they were among the trees, it would be a simple matter to cover their tracks. Given even a short headstart, they could soon reckon themselves free of any real chance of pursuit. And with Heft's skills, she had no doubt at all they could track Thag. Beyond that she refused to think. She would find Thag and make him safe. Somehow.

"Heft," Hana whispered, "we should—"

She saw a pale, slim figure lifted bodily from out of the crowd and placed directly below Shil on the Rock of Judgment. The Weakling Stranger looked at once familiar and terrified. Why he should look familiar she did not know; despite her special love for Shiva, most Weakling Strangers looked the same to her. But the expression of terror was easier to understand. The anger of those who surrounded Shil was all too clear.

"—go now while we have the chance," Hana concluded.

"We go," Heft said.

"Keep your head down!" Hana whispered urgently to Doban. They moved out together from the shelter of the bush.

Someone in the crowd around the Rock of Judgment began a muttered chant of "*Kill . . . kill . . . kill. . . .*" So far it had not been taken up by any of the others, but Hana supposed that was only a matter of time. Had Thag still been chief, she would have moved to stop that nonsense quickly. With emotions running high, persuading the clan to kill the Weakling Stranger would be all too easy—and emotions always seemed to be running high about one thing or another. But Hana knew that to murder a Weakling Stranger was to invite attack by their tribes, whose magic was too strong for any clan to resist. To murder a Weakling Stranger would be declaration of war, and a war the clan must lose.

Still, she had more important things to worry about just now. Doubtless somebody else would damp down the growing rage. Perhaps Shil might prove himself a sensible chief in this respect, although she greatly doubted it.

"Quickly," Heft urged, making for the edge of the clearing.

"Quickly," Hana echoed to Doban. She took his hand to encourage him to follow. They began to run, crouching, after Heft.

"I am friend," the Weakling Stranger said, his mouth twisting. "Take me to your chief. I am friend of Thag."

Hana stopped so quickly that Doban almost cannoned into her. This creature was a friend of Thag's? His protestations would do him little good here. Already Shil was growling in his throat at the mere mention of Thag's name. And his bullyboys, catching the mood, were raising their clubs with ill-concealed menace. How could a Weakling Stranger be a friend of Thag? Thag's only Stranger friend was Shiva, who was friend to all the clan. Did he come from Shiva? Had Shiva sent him with a message?

"Come," Heft urged, his voice puzzled and urgent. "Come quickly."

But Hana, locked by indecision, did not come. Instead she stared across the clearing at the panic-stricken Weakling Stranger. Why did he claim to be a friend of Thag's?

Gently at first, but with increasing ferocity, it began to snow.

13

Mamar Shivers

The world was white. Light reflected from the snowfield dazzled her eyes and might have left her blind had it not been for the small protection of the hood. As it was, she grew increasingly confused, unable for long moments to decide which direction was up and which was down, let alone which direction was south.

When the confusion gripped her, she stopped and turned and looked to find her own tracks in the snow. That trail led north and helped her establish her bearings again. But should it snow, even a light fall, her tracks would vanish and she would have nothing to guide her.

Mamar's Kingdom was the most desolate place she had ever known, the most desolate place she had ever imagined. It was flat, bleak, featureless and chill. Areas of hard, rocky frozen ground alternated with snowfields, which, when she entered them, stretched from horizon to horizon. So far she had been lucky, for the weather remained kind. But should it snow even lightly, she doubted she would survive. She had trekked miles beyond counting without sight of shelter. There was still no sign of the mountains, so it was unlikely she would find the village this day. Even if it did not snow, what would she do when night fell?

She thought she could build a snow shelter, a lair burrowed in the snow where she could hide until the daylight came. Such shelters were warm, as she knew, even without fire, for she doubted she would be able to build one big enough to allow her to light a fire. But there was a problem. In snowfall, such a shelter might become buried completely, and while a tribe could always cooperate in rescue, one girl alone might have difficulty digging herself out. So a snow shelter might transform itself into a trap. A cave would be better if she could find a cave.

A thought occurred to her unbidden. Suppose the Crone grew impatient? How long did she have to complete her return? Perhaps she had less time than she thought. And if she did fail her test, if she arrived safely back with the tribe but arrived too late, what then? She would not be Crone, of course, but would her tribe still welcome her? Perhaps she would be exiled, driven out to die like the women in the icy tomb.

The thoughts generated fear and drove her tired legs to greater effort. For a time she found herself staggering, half running through the snow.

She slowed eventually, pulled back by exhaustion, and plodded onward in a dogged trek that carried her painfully across the featureless landscape.

She heard a noise like the breaking of a branch and felt, or thought she felt, a brief but violent tremor underneath her feet. Instinct halted her at once, nostrils flaring as she sought scent. She had seen nothing, not even small game, since she had left the safety of the cave, but that did not mean Mamar's Kingdom was empty of life. Had she herself not seen a vision of the great cat Saber here? And if Saber lived, there must be game to hunt. And if there was game to hunt, there were other hunters. However, the shaking of the ground had felt more like the approach of a mammoth herd, except that it had not lasted long enough and there was no noise.

No scent reached her as she spun around in search of movement. There was nothing, no break in the flat white surface save for her own tracks. She held still, chest heaving, her breath fogging before her, her senses fully alert.

It came again, louder this time and closer: a sharp, staccato report like the snapping of a thick, dry branch. This time the ground beneath her feet did not tremble but actually shifted in a fluid motion, as a raft might do when carried by a wave. And suddenly, from the corner of her eye, she saw something rushing toward her.

Shiva dropped her bundle, spun and reached for the flint knife all in a single movement, fiercely determined to defend herself against Saber himself if need be. But it was not Saber who bore down on her, nor any other living creature. The ground itself was opening, and a widening crack sped swiftly in her direction, splitting the snowfield like a wound.

For the barest instant Shiva stared, mind racing, unable to understand what she was seeing. Then, in a rush, it came to her. She had been walking on snow-covered ice, a frozen lake, and now the ice had cracked.

Shiva ran. As she ran, the ground before her transformed itself into a spider's web of cracks and a horrid rumbling filled her head. She felt horribly afraid, as if fear were a living creature that had hunted her and caught her. With the fear came sharp confusion. Even if she walked the frozen surface of a lake, why had it broken now? The world was so cold, the ice must be many feet thick, strong enough to support her and her whole tribe, or even a mammoth herd.

The ground shook. Shiva fell, pitched forward by the terrible shaking.

And suddenly she knew. Mamar, God of Ice, jealous of the sanctity of his domain, was shivering with rage against her. It happened sometimes, as she knew from the old women of the tribe. When the gods were enraged, the earth shook. Sometimes they breathed fire and smoke from out of the ground. Sometimes they boiled mud.

But when they did not breathe fire or boil mud, their anger did not last long, the old ones said. So there was seldom too much danger unless you were among trees, or beneath a high place that could produce a landslide. Or on a frozen lake, Shiva thought.

The noise ceased, the shaking ceased. Shiva, thrown flat on her face, stood up slowly. The ground beneath her feet still moved, but smoothly, as if she were floating on a broad, slow river. The shaking ground had cracked the frozen surface of the lake and broken it into a series of floes. She looked around to find she was standing on one of them, no more than fifteen paces wide. She could see the dark, chill depths of water welling up on either side.

She had to get off the lake. If Mamar shook himself again, she could be thrown into those waters; and even if she escaped again—which would not be easy—she knew that getting soaked here in the open would mean she would be dead long before she could create a fire to give her warmth.

The floe on which she stood floated no more than five feet from the next, but the gap was widening. Without thought, Shiva jumped. She ran across the next floe and jumped again, crossing the narrow gap easily. But then the ice moved, so that the crack between this floe and the next widened alarmingly, forcing her to move sideways, then double back. She hopped from floe to floe, sometimes moving south, sometimes west, sometimes east, sometimes back north, always seeking the edge of the frozen lake.

Although the effort was exhausting, progress became increasingly easy, for the floes tended to drift closer together with time, and already she

151

could see a skin of new ice beginning to reform. Eventually, a great many paces distant from the nearest remaining crack, she decided she might be safe. She stood, chest heaving, staring back toward the lake. As she did so, Mamar shook himself again, sending tremors though her body, but the ground beneath her feet did not crack. She was clear of the ice.

She was also lost. The realization hit her at once. She had doubled back so often, she could no longer decide which was north and which was south. Worse still, she had lost her pack: Her store of food and firewood had been swallowed by the lake.

Shiva stood quite still, a small dark speck in a flat cold world. She could find south again when the sun set, simply by watching the light patterns of the sky. But until then? She could not simply stand still. The chill would eat through her clothing and leach the warmth from her blood. And besides, she had no time to waste. But if she set off in the wrong direction, she would waste more time still. She had no shadow stick, no back trail; and now the sun was hidden by the gray-white covering of cloud. Which way was south?

A memory of the Ordeal by Poison crept into her mind: the bowls before her, each looking like

152

the rest, only one from which she might safely drink, and the voice of her dead mother urging her to chose *that* one, the one on the end. She had been well guided by the voice then, for she had survived the Ordeal. And later, while she huddled over her first fire, the voice of her mother had come again, urging her to explore the cave.

"Mother?" Shiva whispered.

Nothing. There was no sound but the low moan of the wind.

"Mother . . ." Shiva said again. She turned hesitantly. "Is this south, Mother?"

Still nothing. She was alone.

Alone and growing chill. She could not afford to stand still here in the open without shelter. She would have to trust her instincts, select a direction and hope she was not plunging back into the frozen heartland. She closed her eyes, took a deep breath, made her best judgment and set off again. After an hour, it began to snow lightly.

14

Death in the Forest

"You've been very bad, Thag," Metrak said, grinning. "You've killed Led. And I think you may have killed Dag the Flint Chipper as well."

He might not actually have killed Led, Thag thought, although it was not for want of trying. He had certainly killed Dag the Flint Chipper. And he would kill Metrak, given half a chance. And he would kill Shil, especially Shil.

Thag knew, though, that he would not kill Shil, who was far away and now chief of the clan. The fact was that he would not kill anybody, ever again, for he was utterly exhausted, quite unable to move and in hideous pain. If there was any killing to be done, Metrak would do it. Vaguely, Thag hoped he would do it quickly. Once he was dead, Thag thought, the pain would stop.

"Chief Shil will not be pleased with you," Metrak said, voice gloating. He was a man who liked to gloat. Up to now he had had little enough to gloat about, but all that had changed when his friend Shil had become chief.

Thag lay quite still, his breath catching. He wished he had not fallen on Led, who made an uncomfortable cushion. Sharp bits of Led, his elbow and knee, were sticking into him, polishing the pain so that it danced and sparkled, blood red, before his eyes.

Thag felt himself sinking. It was a curiously pleasant sensation, for it took him from the pain. He found, quite suddenly, that many things that had once concerned him did not concern him anymore. The deeper he sank, the farther he moved away from the pain, the more comfortable he became. He was no longer aware of Led beneath him. It was as if he were lying on a comfortable and comforting pile of grass or straw.

He noticed strange things were happening to his vision. There was darkness creeping in around the edges. He stared at the darkness, noting how it framed Metrak's gloating face. He liked the way it crept, for soon—or eventually—it would creep all the way and hide Metrak's ugly features altogether. When that happened, Thag would be dead. But that did not matter. Nothing mattered when you were dead.

He would be born again, Thag thought. He had not thought much about that before now because he had not found himself engaged in dying before now. When he died, they would take his body and bind it with his knees bent and paint it with red ochre. They would place it facing eastward in a cavern tomb and cover it with forest flowers. And his soul would fly beyond the rising sun in search of a baby about to be born. His soul would join with that baby, and he would be born again in the clan and grow big and strong.

A terrible thought struck him. What if the baby was a girl? If the baby was a girl, he could never grow up strong enough to challenge Shil and once again become the chief of his clan. He sighed. It did not matter. Nothing mattered once you died.

"Chief Shil will order your death." Metrak grinned. "Chief Shil will—" He stopped, frowning, as Thag closed his eyes. "Here," he said in sudden panic, "what do you think you're doing?"

Thag's eyes flickered briefly open. "I'm dying," he whispered softly through a rattle in his throat.

"You're dying? You can't die!" Metrak roared. "I won't let you die! You have to come back with me. You have to come back to the clan so I can tell them how you killed Led and Dag the Flint Chipper and how I bravely captured you. You have to come back so Shil can show everyone the rotten things you've done and have you put to death. You can't die now. It isn't *fair*!"

At least, Thag thought, he had stopped gloating. He gasped as Metrak shook him violently, causing the pain to come spilling through the darkness like a flood. He groaned.

"You aren't dead yet!" spat Metrak. "No you aren't, Thag, not by a long shot! You were always strong. You used to be the strongest in the clan. I didn't hit you that hard. A little tap on the head and a few broken bones—what's that to a man like you? You'll make it back to the caverns. You'll make it back and Shil can have you put to death and I'll be a hero, yes indeed."

Metrak was trying to pull him to his feet. The pain erupted once again throughout his body, but he ignored it, for it felt like someone else's pain. What he could not ignore was his weakness. Even if he had wished to stand, he could not have done so. Swimming in and out of darkness, Thag realized he was too heavy, too heavy for poor old Metrak to drag him anywhere. Poor old Metrak. He would not bring Thag back to the caverns

157

alive. He would not be a hero.

Poor old Metrak dropped him so that he fell in a heap on the forest floor. There was no pain. The darkness had almost closed around him now, and he was scarcely aware of his surroundings. In place of the pain there was a numbness that crept through his body, soothing the pain, hiding the pain.

Metrak was making something. Thag retained just enough interest to watch and wonder vaguely what it was all about. Metrak was breaking branches from the trees and weaving them together to form a mat. But why would Metrak want a mat? Sometimes—not often but sometimes—people of the clan wove a mat like that to sleep upon. It was a very large mat, certainly large enough for Metrak to sleep upon, so perhaps that was what it was for. Thag lost interest and closed his eyes. It did not matter.

Metrak was moving him. Thag tried to protest and the pain returned, so he stopped protesting and allowed it all to happen. Metrak was moving him onto the mat. Metrak was pulling him along the forest floor.

That was all right. Metrak was dragging him on the mat back to the caverns of the clan. When they reached the caverns, Metrak would be a hero and Shil would condemn Thag to death for something or other. Everyone would be happy. Metrak would be happy because he would be a hero. Shil would be happy because he had gotten rid of Thag once and for all. Thag would be happy because he would be dead and searching for a new, young body that had neither pain nor numbness in it.

Doban would not be happy, his mind muttered grimly. His son, Doban, would not be happy at Thag's death. His friend Heft the Hunter would not be happy at Thag's death. Most important of all, his mate, Hana, would not be happy at Thag's death.

Thag opened his eyes and fought back the darkness. He was wrapped around with roughly twisted creepers that tied him loosely to the woven mat of branches so he would not fall off as Metrak dragged it bumpily along the forest trails.

Thag swam upward out of the darkness and felt the pain return, more fiercely than ever before. His shoulder and arm pained him mightily, hotly. His head pained him, a dull, thumping pain. His chest pained him when he breathed. Even his legs pained him, although he could not remember having injured them.

Thag pushed through the pain. It was too soon

159

for him to die. He would not die, not here in the forest, not back at the caverns condemned by Shil, the false chief of the clan. He would push back the pain and he would *live*!

But he could not push back the weakness. The twisted vines were loosely tied, but he could not break free of them. And had he broken free of them, he doubted he could stand. Stretched helpless on the pallet, he stared at Metrak's hairy back as Metrak dragged him through the forest.

Metrak stopped eventually, tiring of his burden. As he turned, he must have noticed Thag's eyes were open, for he said, "Feeling better, are you? Good."

Thag said nothing. He scratched feebly at the vines that tied him.

"Too tight?" Metrak asked, frowning. He was obviously deeply concerned with Thag's comfort, at least until he could bring him back alive. He leaned down and eased the makeshift ropes. "Better?" Metrak asked in the tone of one who does not really expect much of an answer.

Perhaps, Thag thought, if he lay still long enough and ignored the pain, his strength would return. But then what? He would have to lie still for weeks, for months perhaps, before his whole strength would return. However much he lay still just now, he would scarcely reclaim enough strength to lift one uninjured arm, let alone escape from Metrak or wrest his old power back from Shil. It was stupid to imagine he could really do anything at all except lie in his cloud of pain and wait for Metrak to drag him home, wait for Shil to order his execution.

He shivered. Or rather, something made him shiver, something shivered through him. It was a strange sensation, as if his body, suddenly, was no longer his own.

There was a deep, throaty growling, as much in his head as in his ears, as if some monster far beyond the mammoth in dimensions were stalking through the forest. Metrak heard it too, for he stood stock-still, head tilted, obviously listening.

"What—?" Metrak asked, glancing about him nervously.

The growling broke over them like a sea wave. To his astonishment, Thag felt the ground move, throwing him sideways so forcefully that, with loosened bonds, he almost slipped from the pallet. Intermingled with the growling, he heard a series of sharp cracks and an ominous hissing that grew louder by the instant. He looked around him, sudden panic momentarily overcoming his exhaustion and his pain.

The forest was shaking. Shaking fiercely as if gripped by some mighty wind. Thag tried to call out but could not.

Metrak spun around in terror, desperately seeking the source of the danger.

A tree was falling. No, not one tree but many, forest giants crashing down in a ferocity of noise and movement. They cracked and fell as if some invisible leviathan lumbered through the trails, snapping them like twigs in its passage.

Metrak dropped into a protective crouch, his eyes wide.

Thag watched as the great tree toppled. It was falling directly toward them and there was nothing he could do. At that instant he felt no fear, merely sorrow that he should have survived so long only to die now, crushed beneath a falling tree.

The tree fell, its spreading branches ripping through the branches of its neighbors in a creaking, cracking, tidal wave of sound.

15

Confrontation

Something had gone badly wrong. They had understood. He was certain they had understood. "Take me to your chief," he had said. "I am friend. I am friend of Thag." They had heard him and they had understood. Yet they had taken him not to Thag but to another ogre altogether, a little smaller, not quite so ugly, but just as quarrelsome and twice as spiteful.

This bad-tempered creature who sat upon a rock and walked with a limp, had shrieked and screamed and gesticulated until he had the whole clan half mad with excitement. Then they had dragged Hiram off to the dark and the damp and the chill of the deep caves and left him bound with gut and strips of skin.

He had lain in darkness for perhaps an hour

when he actually felt the ground shake. It shook again, causing his whole body to tremble as if in the grip of fear. Hiram held his breath. What was happening? He heard the guard scramble to his feet and move away, but then there was the sound of the guard returning and the whisper of his breathing as he settled down again.

For a long while Hiram remained still, waiting for something to happen, trying to guess what had happened. Eventually, cautiously, he began to explore his bonds. They were tightly tied, impossible to break. He felt he had been in the darkness forever and suspected he would remain in the darkness for a long time more. What did they plan to do with him?

Hiram thought he knew the answer to that question. Ogres had a taste for human brains. Everybody said so—except Shiva. Shiva insisted all the talk about brain eating was nonsense, but he knew better. Not that he had ever seen an ogre eating human brains, but everybody said they did, and he believed it. It was obvious to Hiram he was being *stored*. He had been tied up and left in the deep cave to wait for dinnertime.

Hiram did not know what to do. He had been captured by ogres once before and escaped in the confusion when they had fought among themselves. There was no chance of his escaping now. He was bound, hand and foot, in the deep warren of caverns that riddled the cliff.

But if he did not do something, his brains would be eaten. If he did not do something, he would never find Shiva. Hiram began to work silently to loosen his bonds. It was tough going. The ogres who had tied him had done a good job.

He stopped, listening. He had heard a grunt in the darkness, followed by a dull thud. The sounds came from just beyond the entrance near where the ogre guard was squatting. Hiram wondered what they meant.

Something was coming into the cave. An *ogre* was coming into the cave. His nose told him that at once, just as it told him the ogre was not the guard, who had a distinctive body scent—the familiar musky smell was underlaid by the aroma of damp earth. This new ogre did not smell the same at all. Who was it? Why was it coming for him?

There was only one possible answer. It was coming to take him to dinner.

Panic flooded Hiram's body and he managed to jerk one arm completely free. He felt the looming warmth of the ogre as the huge beast settled beside him. He struck out desperately.

The ogre grunted in surprise at Hiram's fist. A

leathery hand gripped Hiram's wrist and held it so firmly, he could not move at all.

"It is important we are quiet," the ogre whispered.

"Let me—" Hiram stopped. The ogre had spoken in *human* tongue! It was impossible. Yet he had heard the words, though heavily accented and a little growly.

"I am Doban," the ogre said. "I have come to help you to escape."

Hiram knew that name. Doban was the *ogre* boy who had once saved Shiva from a wolf. Doban was Shiva's special friend. Most important of all, Doban was the son of Thag, the ogre chief.

"I am friend," Hiram said eagerly. "Take me to your chie—to your father. I am friend of Thag."

"My father Thag is gone," growled Doban fiercely. "You be quiet now!" He released Hiram's wrist and reached out broad, strong hands to tug at the remaining bonds.

This could not be Doban, Hiram thought. Doban was a boy, younger than Hiram himself, younger even than Shiva. Hiram had seen him once and carried the memory of an ugly, muscular ogre child. The ogre beside him now was huge, huge almost as Hiram's memory of Thag. Could ogres grow so quickly?

166

"Doban," Hiram whispered in his own tongue, "I have to find Heft the Hunter."

"Quiet now!" warned Doban. "The guard sleeps, but there may be others."

"Sleeps?" Hiram echoed.

"I sleep him with his club," Doban explained clumsily, although the meaning was clear enough. He placed his mouth close to Hiram's ear and whispered angrily, "Quiet. You be quiet." He tugged violently, and the bonds snapped.

"I have to find Heft the Hunter to find Shiva!" Hiram said, climbing to his feet.

"You look for Shiva?" Doban asked.

"She's lost," Hiram said, not wanting to go into a detailed explanation. "I need to find Hef—"

"Heft the Hunter waits outside," Doban cut him off. His hand reached out of the darkness to swallow Hiram's own. "I lead. You follow and be quiet."

Hiram followed. He could see nothing in the darkness, but knew well that Doban could, for ogres had astonishing night vision. Eventually they reached the upper levels where enough light filtered through to allow him to see. The looming shape of Doban carried a wicked-looking club, possibly the one he had used to "sleep" the guard. He looked amazingly like his father, Thag,

167

a long way from the boy Hiram remembered.

There were sounds of ogres approaching, and Doban pulled him into a crevice where they huddled together until the danger was past. As the sounds receded, they crept from the crevice and moved quickly along the tunnels until at length they emerged among some tangled bushes at one side of the clearing. There were two ogres crouching half hidden in the undergrowth, waiting for them.

Hiram recognized one of them at once, the white-haired ogre female who, he remembered, had bullied Chief Thag unmercifully and was, as Shiva had explained, his wife and Doban's mother. The female came quickly toward them. She said something to Doban, but too quickly for Hiram to make out the words, then turned directly to him and spoke in his tongue.

"You are a friend of Thag?" she asked.

Something told Hiram not to lie. "Not exactly a friend," he said. "I am a friend of Shiva, who is a friend of Th—"

"Yes, yes," Hana said impatiently. "I thought that might be it. Why are you here? I remember you; you were here before. Thag carried you."

Hiram nodded dumbly. He swallowed. "I need—They sent Shiva away, I don't know why,

168

somewhere awful, into Mamar's Kingdom. I could not track her there, so—"

"Are you Shiva's mate?" Hana interrupted him, frowning.

Hiram blushed crimson. "No, not at all. I asked her once, but—No, I—"

"Good," Hana said. "Nobody should marry—it brings nothing but trouble. Who sent Shiva into the frozen world?"

"The tribe," Hiram said. "The women of the tribe."

"Why did they do that? She will die in the frozen world."

"I don't know why they did. They won't tell me. I know she'll die there, but I couldn't track her after the snow." The words began to tumble out of him, faster and faster. "But Shiva told me of a great ogr—of a great tracker from your people called Heft the Hunter, and I came here to find him so he could help me find Shiva, because—"

The second ogre moved across and stuck his face no more than an inch from Hiram's own so that Hiram stopped speaking. "Ma eftuntrr," the ogre growled.

"What's he say?" Hiram whispered.

"He says he is Heft the Hunter," Hana told him

169

shortly. She glanced around her. "I like Shiva. So does Heft. We will help you find her if we can, but first we must find Thag."

"Thag?" Hiram looked at her uneasily.

"The clan has a new chief now," said Hana blankly. "He sent Thag away. As you search for Shiva, we search for Thag. If we do not find him, he may"—she gave a sidelong glance to Doban—"get into trouble." She looked around her. Hiram, peering through the bushes, noticed the clearing was almost empty. "You will come with us," Hana said in the sort of tone the tribal elders used when they did not want any argument.

"I must find Shiva!" Hiram told her, his voice bordering on panic.

"You can't stay here," Hana said. "Didn't you hear what Shil said?"

"Shil?"

"The new chief."

Hiram stared at his feet. "I couldn't understand him," he muttered.

"He wants to kill you as a warning to your people not to come into the forest." Hana sighed. "He is an idiot, of course, but that does not make things any easier for you. If you stay here, you will die. But if you wish, you can go off alone. Doban and Heft and I go to seek Thag."

Without Heft the Hunter, he had no chance of finding Shiva. But once they found Thag, he might persuade them to help him look for her. "I shall go with you," he said. He looked from one to the other, wondering if he had taken leave of his senses. A few hours before, he could not have imagined himself going anywhere with three ogres.

"We go now," Hana said. She stepped out of hiding. Heft followed her at once. Hiram took a deep breath and moved from the bushes.

As he did so, there was a sudden commotion on the edge of the clearing, an excited shouting that reverberated all across the cliff face and called ogre after ogre from the multitude of entrances. Without thought, Hiram dived back for cover and walked directly into one of Shil's men emerging from an opening in the cliff face.

16

Return

She was in the forest. Even as it happened, she could scarcely believe it. One moment she was lost in the storm, colder and more frightened than she had ever been. The next she was in the shelter of the tall, familiar trees. And while snow still fell and the wind still blew, suddenly she could see more than a foot or two ahead. Now there were places that would protect her: hollow tree trunks, abandoned burrows, even a tangle of undergrowth that formed a natural roof.

Shiva stopped, allowing her exhausted body to take a moment's rest while she gave grateful thanks to the Mother. She knew the forest, knew its trails and its signs. She had friends here who would welcome her to their caverns and their hearthfires, friends who would give her meat.

Her stomach grumbled at the thought, but she ignored it. Hungry though she was, she remained a long way from starvation. For now it was enough to know she would live. She would find her way back to her tribe.

She wondered if she should find shelter and wait out the storm. She was tired, very tired, and it might make sense to hide away until the worst of it blew over. But while there would be little problem finding a shelter, she could not make a fire. Her firestone was gone, lost in the lake, her resinous tinder gone with it. Without the two, she could never make fire in this dripping forest, not unless she found a cave somehow. She might as well try to find the caverns of the clan, where there would be fire to welcome her.

She decided to compromise. In less than fifteen minutes she had found the remnants of an ancient fallen tree and crawled inside its hollow trunk. The air was damp and overlaid with fur scents from small animals, but nothing that carried any hint of threat. She lay down, curled in upon herself to preserve body heat and attempted, unsuccessfully, to sleep.

But if sleep would not come, at least she rested; and eventually, fitfully, she dozed, entering that curious half world she sometimes thought must be like the dreamtime where she was partly aware of her physical surroundings, partly in another place altogether. At one point she thought she heard the Crone's voice, dry and somber, but could not make out the words.

Shiva snapped back to normal consciousness with a start, wondering how long she had been curled up in the hollow log. She crawled out, aware of the chill and stiffness in her body but feeling distinctly better for the rest. Snow was still falling, but the wind had dropped, and it seemed likely that the storm was passing. She stretched and looked around her, searching for clansigns. The old trunk in which she had sheltered was not the only fallen tree in her immediate surroundings. A number of far younger trees had toppled, some fallen to the forest floor, others leaning, caught up precariously in their companions. The forest had obviously suffered when Mamar had tried to shake her from his back. She was surprised she had not noticed it before.

The damage might have obliterated some signs, but not all of them, for the forest carried a multitude of indicators left by her secret friends. No one of the clan ever entered new territory without leaving a mark, and for those who had the eyes to see them, clansigns told much. She

174

followed the practice she had been taught and circled in a slow, careful, outward spiral, her eyes darting everywhere until, eventually, she found what she was looking for.

It was a small thing, a twig broken in a certain way. It might have snapped when one of the small forest deer brushed by, but Shiva knew it had not. This twig was broken deliberately by one who hunted with the clan, and its lie pointed back toward the caverns he called home.

Shiva trotted off without a moment's hesitation, her heart lighter than it had been since the women had called for her in the night and taken her to the Ordeal by Poison. It seemed like another age now, another lifetime, like a fireside tale about the dreamtime. How many things had changed for her since then! And how many would continue changing when she made her way back to her tribe! She would be Crone. It was almost unimaginable, yet here in the forest she began to imagine it. *She would be Crone.* Not right away, of course, but when the present Crone had taught her the secrets of Cronecraft. She, Shiva, would walk in the deep caves, paint the pictures of power, work the ancient magics. Her name would be known not only in the Shingu tribe, but beyond, in all the tribes.

Shiva stopped. Something had happened here, something violent. She sniffed, seeking scent, and as the wind changed briefly caught the smell of a body. She pushed forward and broke into a clearing. She saw the body at once—heart pounding she ran forward. Who was it? Which of the clan? She turned the head and looked into the broad face with its huge jaw. With a sudden flooding of relief she knew she had never set eyes on this clansman before, at least not as far as she could remember.

The relief proved short-lived. All around her were the clear signs of a vicious fight, one that this unfortunate had lost. The fatal blow had been struck by a club, which was a clan weapon. But why? There was always bickering between the men of the clans, always arguments, often scuffles and fistfights: It was the clan way. But murder was almost unknown.

She bent down to study the ground more carefully. Someone else had lain here, close to the corpse she had found. Carefully she scuffed away the covering of snow and found what she expected: the traces of a body dragged. She circled cautiously. And there it was, despite the snow—a trail of blood.

Moving with swift determination now, she

began to track the blood trail. It was not difficult. Whoever was being dragged had been injured and was bleeding.

In no more than a moment she realized the blood trail led the way that she herself had been traveling: toward the caverns of the clan. It followed the clansign pointers with as little deviation as a hunter heading home.

Shiva trotted like a hunter herself, no longer aware of the chill in her bones and the tiredness in her limbs. Her attention was focused on the blood trail, her mind creating dreadful visions. One clansman dead, another dying. Who knew but that the clansman dying might be one of her special friends?

Shiva found herself running, almost in panic, seized by a frightful foreboding. Everything about the forest felt wrong. The very trees themselves cried out to her, warning that her world contained terrors even beyond those she had already met. All around her were the clear signs of the recent quake: the broken branches, the teetering, shattered trees.

There was something up ahead. She could see the huge tree fallen, the body trapped beneath. Another of the clan! He was dead for certain, his body crushed by the weight of branch and trunk.

As she came close enough to see the features, contorted though they were from pain and death, she recognized him at once. It was Metrak, another of Thag's clan, a sullen man as she remembered him and one she did not know well, but she felt regret rising in her just the same. She loved the clan, loved the great growling, bad-tempered men, loved the sharper, smaller, faster-moving women. The death of any clansperson saddened her, however fleeting their acquaintance.

Just beyond the tree lay Thag. He was untouched but surely dead, eyes wide and staring, black blood oozing from one side of his open mouth.

"Thag!" screamed Shiva. She clawed her way through the branches of the fallen tree, climbed nimbly as a monkey over the massive trunk, reached him in a moment and was weeping in fear and panic as she knelt beside the great, still body.

There was no doubt in her mind but that he was dead. The falling tree had missed him by no more than a foot or two, yet his skin had the pallor of death, his body the awesome stillness of death. His face, so beautiful, so ugly, wore a strangely calm expression. She looked at the blood oozing from his wounds.

A dead body did not bleed. She had known that for years. Hurriedly, she pulled back the skins and placed one ear against his chest. There remained the faintest heartbeat.

She stood up, her mind racing. If he was still alive now, he would not remain alive for long. She had to get him back to his home caverns, back to warmth and Hana, who could brew healing herbs. He must have rest and food and shelter if there was to be any hope of his survival. Yet there was no way he could walk: He was not even conscious.

She would have to get help! If she followed the signs and ran to the caverns, she could guide men back to carry him.

But to leave Thag even for a short time, helpless in the forest, was to invite disaster. Even now the scent of his blood was calling loudly to every wolf and predator around. Somehow she would have to get him back to the caverns, and quickly.

She could not carry him. Tough though she was, there was no way she could lift so large a body; and in any case she suspected an attempt to haul him to his feet might kill him. But there was one other possibility. He lay on a mat of woven branches, tied and harnessed with twisted vines. Metrak must have been dragging him back when the tree fell.

Shiva shook her head violently as if to dismiss doubt. Without further thought, she looped the vines across her chest, then uttering a silent prayer to the Mother, braced herself and pulled.

He did not move.

Shiva took a deep breath and pulled again. She felt the strain on her hamstrings, her shoulders and her back. Thag was immovable. She pulled again, heart pounding, feeling the sudden shooting pains as her muscles protested at the effort. There was just the barest trembling; then Thag's makeshift litter moved.

Shiva lurched forward, her whole being concentrated on the effort to drag her friend's unconscious body. Now that it had begun to move, it was a little easier to keep it moving, but the strain was still enormous. In only a few paces her back began to ache as if it were on fire, and her legs developed a constant trembling. She ignored it all, half closing her eyes and concentrating only on one thing: She had to get Thag to safety quickly.

She had no idea how far she was from the clearing with its towering cliff face riddled with the caverns of the Clan. She had no idea how far she traveled, sweat pouring from her body despite the cold, dragging the vast bulk of Thag behind her. In a short while she hardly remembered what she was doing, only that she must continue to place one foot before the other. In time she could no longer see the signs but simply stumbled forward, driven by some instinct that was stronger than her desire to lie down and rest.

Her breath rasped in her body. Soon it seemed she could go no further without rest. Yet she knew if she once stopped to rest, she no longer had the strength to get Thag moving again. It was pull and pull or stop and watch him die. She pulled.

And suddenly, scarcely aware of where she was, what she was doing, she burst into the clearing. As she sank to her knees, she heard, as if from a great distance, the shouts of the clansmen who had recognized her burden.

17

Combat

Thag! Hana froze in her tracks. It was Shiva, friend to the clan, and behind her, stretched out on a woven mat of branches and dragged by her, was Thag.

"Thag!" Hana screamed. Her paralysis broke, and she began to run forward.

But already Thag and Shiva were half surrounded as alerted members of the clan streamed from the caverns. Hana had caught no more than a glimpse of Thag, her mate, but a glimpse was enough. If he was not dead, he was so close to death that only the most urgent action could save him.

She burst through the crowd around him like a rampaging bear. Shiva knelt on the frozen ground, head bowed, chest heaving, breath pluming from her open mouth. She looked exhausted, but she was young and would recover quickly.

Thag was a different story. His great body lay motionless on the pallet without so much as a movement of his chest to show there was still life in him. There was blood around his mouth, across his face, matted in his tangled hair. He looked pale as a corpse.

Hana knelt and reached out to touch him. He was cold as rock. In sudden desperation, she began to pull away the skins to search for a heartbeat.

"He's still alive," Shiva panted. "Needs warm . . . rest . . . healing—"

Hana accepted her words at once. She had known Shiva since the day the Weakling Stranger girl had returned her boy Doban to the clan. Shiva had a strength and competence far beyond her years. If Shiva said Thag still lived, Hana would not waste time confirming it. She spun around.

"You and you," she ordered, seized by old habits of command, "get him inside to a fire. Cover him well. Make him warm." Her eyes searched out one of the women. "Hot soup," she demanded. She half turned. "I shall dress his wounds myself."

183

"So," a soft voice hissed beside her ear. "Thag has defied my orders and returned!"

Hana found herself staring into the cold black eyes of Shil. He was smiling.

"No one moves," said Shil, and the two men who had started forward instinctively to carry Thag into the caves stopped at once. Shil stared around him arrogantly. "Do you see?" he asked. "Do you see how this outcast defies me? Me, Shil, the rightful chief!" He licked his lips. "Did I not order him to leave the clan? Did I not banish him? Did I not forbid him to return? Yet here he is." He gestured, his face taking on the expression of one who was forced to endure a bad smell.

"He is injured!" Hana screamed. "He is nearly dead!"

But Shil ignored her. "I was merciful," he said. "Was I not merciful? Did I not grant this man his life after I had defeated him in a fair fight? I might have killed him then and there, but I was merciful and only sent him away to find another cave. And now he defies me and returns. Worse still"—his eyes turned back to Hana and his smile broadened—"I find his mate has left the caverns against my express order, taking with her—" His gaze searched out Hiram, now seized on either arm by two of Shil's men. "Taking with her this

184

spy sent by the Weakling Strangers!"

Shiva, a little rested now, raised her head. "What has happened here?" she asked Hana softly. Her eyes fell on Hiram and widened. Hiram stared back, mouth open.

"This creature," Shil proclaimed, turning back to the prostrate form of Thag, "has broken Shil's law. For that, if he is not dead already, he must now die!"

Hana flung herself between the body of her mate and Shil. "No!" she spat. "You shall not touch him!"

But Shil, still grinning broadly, waved an airy hand. "Indeed I shall not. But he will die just the same. The clan must obey its chief, and I, Shil, its rightful chief, now order Thag must die."

A burly form pushed through the circle and cuffed aside Shil's nearest guard with a single backswipe of one powerful arm. He leaned forward until his face was no more than an inch from Shil's own. "I am strong!" Doban growled. "I am the strongest of the clan!"

"Doban . . ." Hana whispered. She half moved to stop him, then hesitated. Her boy, her little boy, now stood as tall as Shil and just as broad. There was so much of his father in him. Was it possible he might be what he now claimed?

Shil's grin vanished and he stepped back in alarm. "Seize him!" he ordered. "He threatens your chief!"

But no one moved. From somewhere at the back of the collected crowd, a voice said quietly, "Challenge!" In a moment the word was repeated, then taken up as a chant by another voice and another. "Challenge!" Soon the entire compound was filled with the angry sound.

Shil looked around him desperately. "I am chief," he said. "It is beneath my dignity to fight this boy."

"Fight!" commanded Doban.

"We will get clubs," Shil shouted. "We will—"

His words were cut off as Doban bunched one fist and brought it down on the top of Shil's head. Shil's eyes glazed, and he staggered back briefly.

"Fight! Fight! Fight!" chanted the watching crowd.

With a roar, Shil threw himself forward, arms flailing. Hana sucked in her breath, but Doban simply stepped aside and stuck out one foot so that Shil tripped and went flying. He picked himself up at once and ran again. This time Doban punched him in the throat. Shil staggered back again, clutching his throat and mouthing words that would not emerge.

Hana felt a hand on her arm.

"We must get Thag to heat," Shiva said quietly.

Hana looked at the still body of her mate, then glanced back at her son, now crouched to meet another charge from Shil.

"Doban will win," Shiva whispered. "He knows new ways to fight."

"You taught him?" Hana asked, astounded. She knew how friendly Doban had been over these past years with the Weakling Stranger girl, but she had not suspected this. Shiva nodded.

Between them they began to drag Thag's bulk toward the caverns. As they did so, one of the watching women whispered into Hana's ear, "I will bring soup," and scurried away.

"Thank—" Hana began, but it was already too late. She tugged the mat of branches, wondering how her Thag had come to this. Shil's doing, doubtless, but Shil might soon be in no position to do any further damage. She could still see the fight. Now Doban had gone on the offensive and was charging Shil, head lowered. Hana felt a fierce pride well up in her. Doban would teach the usurper.

Doban's lowered head connected with Shil's stomach, knocking the breath from him and propelling him backward. Shil recovered, mimicking

Doban's head-down charge before Doban could retain his balance.

"Having second thoughts, boy?" Shil crowed. "I taught the father a lesson—now I'll teach a lesson to his pup!" He jumped forward, turned sideways and drove his elbow into Doban's stomach in the same place where he had butted. "Who's strongest now?" Shil taunted. He moved in and clasped his hands together to bring them down on Doban's exposed neck.

Doban straightened with a cave lion's roar, his own fists striking upward under Shil's chin. They connected, snapping back Shil's head violently. They grappled like wrestlers, arms around one another, each straining to throw his opponent on the ground. For a long moment they swayed, locked together, muscles straining. Young though he was, Doban seemed the stronger, for Shil's whole body was bending, contorting. Then, with a darting movement, Shil bit Doban on the ear.

Doban howled in pain and dropped his guard. In an instant, Shil swept back with his heel. They fell together heavily with Doban underneath.

Hana and Shiva reached the cave mouth with Thag. Inevitably, at this season, there was a well-stoked fire no more than a few yards inside. To Hana's surprise there were several clanswomen waiting. Two carried containers of steaming soup. Another was unfolding a skin containing healing herbs. Hana felt a lump well up in her throat.

Outside, Doban pushed up with his entire body so that Shil rolled off him. They both jumped nimbly to their feet, although Shil seemed to be breathing more heavily. All the same, it was Shil who was first to attack again. It was a violent blow that caught Doban on the nose, causing a sudden spurt of blood and sending him reeling. Doban staggered, then fell. Shil jumped and landed with both feet on his unprotected stomach. Doban's eyes rolled, then closed.

The momentum of Shil's movements carried him beyond the supine body of his opponent. He turned, saw Doban had not risen and, for the first time since the fight had begun, broke into his familiar, chilling smile.

"Strongest in the clan, boy?" he asked, panting. "Who's strongest now? Who's strongest now?" He began to walk slowly toward the prostrate Doban.

"Doban!" called someone sharply in the crowd.
"Doban!" called another.
Shil glanced across, lips curling with contempt.
"Do-ban," the crowd began to chant.

189

Shil towered over him, placed one broad foot on Doban's chest. "I am Shil," he called. "I am chief. I am the —"

"Do-ban, Do-ban, Do-ban."

Doban's eyes flickered open, and he seized Shil's leg at the ankle. Shil was thrown backward.

"Do-ban, Do-ban, Do-ban."

Doban dived full length upon him. Shil twisted and broke his grip, and together they rolled almost the full breadth of the clearing before separating. They circled one another warily.

Shil backed off two steps, three, then, without warning, charged. Doban did not even hesitate. They met head-on, but Doban caught him, twisted, threw him, using the momentum of Shil's own charge against him.

"Do-ban, Do-ban, Do-ban," chanted the excited crowd.

Shil remained where he was, crouched kneeling on the ground, head down, chest heaving. Doban turned away from him and stared around. "My father?" he asked.

"In the caverns!" somebody called. "Your mother took him into the caverns!"

Doban had turned toward the caverns when it happened. Og-nar, Shil's man, pushed to the

front of the crowd and, in a single swift and un-
expected movement, threw Shil a heavy club.
Shil caught it, leaped to his feet and launched
himself at Doban's unprotected back.

18

Strongest of the Clan

Shiva emerged from the cavern only yards from the fight as Shil caught the club and started forward. "Doban!" she screamed. "Look out!" Without an instant's thought, she hurled herself forward and leaped on Shil's broad back.

Shil stopped, surprised, and half turned, swinging Shiva's feet clear of the ground. Then he shook himself violently, spinning around to dislodge her. She wrapped her legs around his waist and clung with all her strength.

"I kill!" Shil yelled, and heaved. Shiva's grip slackened momentarily, and she found herself hurled through the air. She landed badly, arched across a half-buried rock. She could scarcely breathe, let alone climb back to her feet.

Shil lumbered toward her. "I kill!" he screamed

again. "I, Shil, your chief, will kill the Weakling Stranger, then I kill Doban, who dares fight me, then I kill Thag, who came back against my orders, then I kill—"

He was insane. It showed clearly in his eyes, in the rage that distorted his features. Shiva stared up at him, knowing he was mad, knowing one blow of that massive club would smash her skull like a gull's egg.

She saw Doban start toward Shil but knew he was too far away to reach him in time. The club was raised. "Die!" snarled Shil.

Hiram struck him like a tiger. From the corner of her eye, Shiva saw the surprised look on the faces of the two clansmen from whom Hiram had broken free. Shil was larger than Hiram, broader, stronger, but Hiram had the advantage of surprise and speed. He drove into Shil's side with such ferocity that Shil actually stumbled and dropped to one knee.

The flare of pain in Shiva's back was dying down a little so that she could move. She rolled off the rock.

Doban was almost upon him as Shil climbed back to his feet, but Shil still held the club. He swung it at Doban's head in imitation of the blow that had bested Doban's father. A burst of booing erupted from the crowd.

Doban ducked, and the club whistled harmlessly above his head. As he did so, he struck out and caught Shil in the chest. Shil pushed forward and struck Doban with his shoulder. Doban staggered back, struck his heel against the same half-buried rock that had injured Shiva, and fell. Shil towered over him and suddenly his face broke into a broad smile. Without a word he raised the club.

Hiram caught his arm from behind.

Shiva watched in astonishment. Incredibly, Hiram held back the blow. She could see the tendons of his neck stand out with the strain. Doban rolled and stood. Og-nar lumbered forward and grabbed Hiram. Hiram released Shil's hand and turned on Og-nar like a cave lion. The club smashed down, but Doban was no longer helpless in its path.

Slowly, painfully, Shiva climbed to her feet.

Before Shil could straighten, Doban struck him forcefully on the side of his head so that he staggered and dropped the club. Shil dived to retrieve it, but Shiva, despite her pain, beat him to it. She seized the weapon and hurled it into the crowd. Doban cast her one brief thankful glance, then muttered at his opponent, "Now you must fight fair. Now we see who is strongest of the clan!" He smashed a bunched fist into Shil's nose. The mad look faded from Shil's eyes. He looked uncertain but he held his ground.

They clashed, grappled, strained. Then Doban was behind him, arm around the thick bull neck. "I am strong," he called. "I am the strongest of the clan." He jerked, and suddenly it was over. Shil slid to the ground, his head rolling at an impossible angle, his eyes open but unseeing. He lay still.

Doban stood over him, panting. For a moment there was silence, stillness. Even Og-nar and Hiram ceased their peculiar battle. Then suddenly the clan erupted. *"Do-ban, Do-ban, Do-ban."* They surged forward and bore a startled Doban aloft on their shoulders, howling as they carried him around the clearing.

The tide of bodies swung toward the cliff face, and as suddenly as the noise had begun, it stopped. Hana, face pale as her hair, was standing in the cave mouth. Those carrying Doban let him down slowly. He stared anxiously into the brown eyes of his little mother. "My father?" he asked.

For a long moment she looked only stunned, exhausted. Her eyes flickered to the crumpled body of Shil that still lay where it had fallen.

Then, as she looked back at Doban, she gave a small, tight, tired smile. "He is breathing. He is warm. Your father will live to see his son made chief of our clan."

19

Shiva's Decision

"I did it!" Hiram was saying, mainly to himself. He shook his head periodically as if he could not believe his own words. "I fought an ogre. I actually fought an ogre!" Then, as if explaining his amazement, he added, "And *lived!*"

Shiva scarcely heard him. She was lost in her own thoughts, and they were thoughts that had nothing to do with Hiram's prowess or her secret friends. Instead, her mind was back in Mamar's Kingdom, in the cavern where she had found herself when she had first awoken from the Ordeal by Poison. She could hear the conversation she had had, repeated over and again.

What is my test? Her own words, spoken softly, fearfully.

Only this. The Crone's voice, dry and somber

197

like a death pronouncement. *To embrace me, kiss me, take the totem pouch from around my neck and place it around your own. That only.*

It seemed so long ago since those words had been spoken, as if she had lived a lifetime in the space of a day. How different it was now. Then she had been lost, alone, chilled to the bone and facing the Mother alone knew what hidden dangers. Now she was warm, well fed by the women of the clan and rested, and had Hiram at her side. Doban, Hana, Heft the Hunter and a small party of clan trackers had escorted them all the way to the forest's edge. Now, in what might be the last brief break before the winter blizzards began in earnest, she and Hiram trudged across the frozen plain toward the foothills and the tribal camp. They would be home in half an hour, an hour at most.

And when they came home, Shiva would be forced to make a frightening decision.

Embrace me, kiss me, take the totem pouch from around my neck and place it around your own. That only. The test, once completed, would set her footsteps firmly on the mystic path, the path that led to her becoming Crone. In Mamar's Kingdom she had thought only of reaching her people, of finding the Hag and carrying out the ordained task. Now, within sight of her goal, she was not so sure.

Shiva was afraid. It was one thing to imagine herself a Crone, yet another to contemplate the reality. Could she really master the magic with which the Hag lived daily?

Hiram had asked her something.

"I'm sorry, Hiram. I wasn't listening."

He looked embarrassed, but that was a familiar-enough state for him. "I was wondering," he said, and hesitated. "I was wondering now that I've proved myself . . ."

"Proved yourself?" Shiva echoed. She often wondered what Hiram was talking about.

He contrived to look hurt. "By fighting an ogre."

"What does that prove?" Shiva asked, genuinely bewildered.

"That I have courage. That I am a man."

"But I've always known that."

"Have you?" Hiram asked, visibly pleased. "Have you really?"

"Everyone's known that," Shiva said, then added as an afterthought, "Except you."

That quieted him for several heartbeats, but before she could lose herself in her thoughts again, he said, "Well, whatever about proving myself, I was wondering if you had reconsidered what I asked you?"

She frowned. "Asked me about what, Hiram?"

"If you would—ah—if you would—ah, if you wou—"

He was going to ask her again to marry him. He always stammered like that when he asked her to marry him.

"If you would—ah—marry me," Hiram concluded finally.

She had, in fact, decided she would marry Hiram, although not for some considerable time. Or rather, she had come to that decision before knowing she might become a Crone. Did Crones marry? The Shingu Crone was ancient beyond belief, and no one ever spoke about her having had a husband. Shiva had never thought about it one way or another, but she thought about it now. Perhaps Crones did not mate. Perhaps that was part of the magic.

But then again, no one had ever mentioned to her that a Crone should not marry. So perhaps she could be Crone and still marry Hiram someday, if Hiram was willing to marry a Crone. She was by no means certain he would be. But she did not even know whether she wanted to become a Crone, whether she married Hiram or not. She was confused.

"Will you?" Hiram repeated.

"Will I what?"

This time there was an edge of annoyance in his voice. "Marry me."

"I don't know," she said.

It threw him into a depression, as it always did, and they walked together in silence. Eventually Shiva asked, "Would you marry a Crone?"

Hiram stopped. "Marry the Crone?"

"Not *the* Crone—*a* Crone."

"There is only one Crone."

"No there isn't," Shiva said. "Every tribe has a Crone. The Barradik, the Tomara, the—"

"I don't want to marry a Barradik," Hiram said with a shudder. "I don't want to marry anybody but you."

"Yes, I know," said Shiva. "I was just wondering if you—" She let the sentence trail. He did not understand, and she did not feel like explaining.

They walked on in silence.

Shiva saw the smoke before they caught sight of the camp, a dense gray-white column that rose from the foothills to point like a finger toward the Mother's heaven.

"They've lit a fire," said Hiram unnecessarily.

The fire was a massive bonfire just outside the

camp, so large the snow was melted across the space of many yards. The women of the tribe were ranged around it, faces painted white, with streaks of red across their mouths and their eyes rimmed black, exactly as they had been on the night they had come to take Shiva to her first Ordeal. Hiram saw them and froze at once, his face expressing a degree of terror he had not shown even among the ogre clan.

But the women ignored Hiram. They watched only Shiva.

Shiva too stopped, waiting. This was, she knew, a welcome. Every eye was on her, every face showed expectation. How had they known she would return at this precise time?

She saw Renka, the tribal chieftain, standing to one side. She saw the entire elder council. And again, as on that night of the Ordeal, there were no men.

Slowly, as if on some silent signal, the women parted, and suddenly Shiva knew the answer to her questions. At the end of the living avenue, half hooded by the massive bearskin, stood the Crone. Her black eyes locked on Shiva's own.

The women waited. They were waiting for her decision. She had survived the Ordeal by Poison. She had survived Mamar's dreadful Kingdom.

202

Now they awaited her decision.

Somehow Shiva knew with absolute certainty that she could choose another course and none would try to influence her, none would ever criticize her. She could go the way of any ordinary woman of the tribe: marry, have children, perhaps one day become an elder of the council. She could turn her back on the magic. She need never strain her mind to learn Cronecraft, need never enter the deep caves where the spirits waited. She could be free of it all. She could take the safe track.

When did you ever take the safe track? asked the figure of the woman she called mother, which rose unbidden in her mind. *When was your destiny that of an ordinary girl?*

Shiva walked between the waiting women until she reached the Crone who was now Hag.

She embraced the Crone. She kissed the Crone. She took the totem bag from around the Crone's neck and placed it around her own.

Epilogue

It was pretty rough in Mamar's Kingdom.

Long before Shiva's time—2.5 million years ago, in fact—ice sheets spread over a quarter of Eurasia and the northern half of North America. Mantles of ice developed in mountain ranges stretching from southern Alaska to Colorado and California; in the European Alps; in the Ural and Caucasus Mountains; in the Himalayas. Mountain glaciers in the South American Andes, the New Zealand Alps, and western Tasmania extended down onto the plains.

As Shiva witnessed in her own time, a mere 30,000 years ago, the ice sheets were almost unimaginably thick—over 8,200 feet (2,500 meters) in Europe, where she lived, over 10,000 feet (3,000 meters) in North America. And with all that ice around, it was bitterly cold: 11–14° Fahrenheit (6°–8° Celsius) colder than today's averages, with something like ten times more dust in the atmosphere.

It got so inhospitable, several species were killed off. Things like the Pliocene horse, several types of fish, the mastodon, the great beavers, the sabertoothed cats, and the ground sloth disappeared everywhere. Llamas, camels, tapirs, horses, and yaks became extinct in North America.

Oddly enough, our distant ancestors seemed to thrive on it. All the early development of humanity came during this period—with the exception of civilization, which came immediately afterward. It's hard enough to understand why, unless you subscribe to that old slogan about "when the going gets tough, the tough get going."

Shiva's people, our ancestors, were certainly tough, and the toughest of them all were the shamans, the Crones. They had to be to survive the initiations.

Initiations are a strange business. You would be hard put to find a single primitive tribe anywhere in the world today that does not make use of initiatory rites. There are initiations that welcome you to manhood or womanhood. There are initiations that admit you into warrior societies. There are initiations without which you can't be a full member of the tribe.

But the most difficult of all initiations are those reserved for anyone who wants to be a shaman. A candidate for shamanic initiation among the Warao peoples of Venezuela, for example, has to find and travel to the manaca palm, a tree that holds a special power.

This journey is not easy. It starts in a wasteland, where the candidate must find a series of water holes that are his only guarantee of survival. Somewhere beyond them he is likely to reach a fearsome abyss, at the bottom of which runs a river infested with alligators and dangerous fish. The area around this chasm is a favorite hunting ground for jaguars, and the Warao firmly believe it is also the haunt of demons who attack anyone attempting to cross.

Should the candidate navigate this abyss safely, he will encounter a number of attractive women who will try to tempt him from his path. If he resists them, he is nearing his goal, but there remains a further guardian to overcome before he reaches it—a giant, aggressive hawk.

Even when he reaches the tree, his troubles are not over. Doors set in the massive trunk open and close so rapidly that anyone attempting to enter runs a severe risk of being crushed. But the candidate will hear the voice of his guide encouraging him to take the chance.

If he does so, he will find himself inside the hollow trunk facing a huge serpent with four colorful horns and a luminous ball on the tip of its tongue. The serpent is served by a second creature, human headed but with a reptile body, that carries away the bones of novices who have failed to clear the doors.

You must be wondering by now if I'm trying to pull your leg. Doors in trees? Horned serpents? Human-headed reptiles? All too true, but not necessarily real. Among the Warao, the candidate prepares for his ordeal by fasting and smoking large, foul-smelling cigars of a native tobacco known to have narcotic properties. Part of his initiation tests are visions brought on by drugs.

Shiva was drugged too at the start of her ordeal. Although she avoided the poison cup, the herbal brew she did drink knocked her out long enough to allow the women of her tribe to carry her to the remote cavern where her tests began.

How much of what followed was real, how much vivid visions, is difficult to determine and perhaps not all that important. The important thing was that the candidate survived, for it was survival that conferred the shamanic Crone power. Shiva did survive and thus became a

Crone herself. She was, in other words, the new shaman of her tribe.

What did this involve? According to *The New Grolier Electronic Encyclopedia*:

> A shaman is a religious or ritual specialist, man or woman, *believed* capable of communicating directly with spirit powers. . . . Shamanic power *is said* to come directly from a supernatural source. . . . A shaman *is said* to be chosen by the spirits. . . . The person *believed* chosen for this calling must undergo an initiatory ordeal. . . . In many cultures the candidate *is believed* to receive during this ordeal a mystical light that enables him or her to see far-off things and to discover the secret places to which lost souls have been taken.

The italics are mine. The author of the entry almost falls over himself to make sure readers won't think he actually accepts any of this nonsense. Whatever they might have believed in the Ice Age, whatever primitives may believe today, anybody with a grain of sense and sophistication knows shamans can't *actually* work magic.

Or can they?